D0394933

NONNA MARIA

and the Case of the Stolen Necklace

NONNA MARIA

and the Case of the Stolen Necklace

A NOVEL

LORENZO CARCATERRA

BANTAM BOOKS
New York

Published in the United States by Bantam Books, an imprint of Random House, a division of Penguin Random House LLC, New York.

Bantam is a registered trademark and the B colophon is a trademark of Penguin Random House LLC.

Library of Congress Cataloging-in-Publication Data
Names: Carcaterra, Lorenzo, author.
Title: Nonna Maria and the case of the stolen necklace / Lorenzo Carcaterra.
Description: First edition. | New York : Bantam Books, [2023]
Identifiers: LCCN 2022036051 (print) | LCCN 2022036052 (ebook) | ISBN 9780593499184 (hardback ; acid-free paper) | ISBN 9780593499191 (ebook)
Subjects: LCGFT: Detective and mystery fiction. | Novels.
Classification: LCC PS3553.A653 N68 2023 (print) | LCC PS3553.A653 (ebook) | DDC 813/.54—dc23/eng/20220728
LC record available at lccn.loc.gov/2022036051
LC ebook record available at lccn.loc.gov/2022036052

Printed in Canada on acid-free paper

randomhousebooks.com

2 4 6 8 9 7 5 3 1

First Edition

Design by Fritz Metsch

This is for my grandson, Oliver, who leaves me with a smile and a warm feeling in my heart each and every day. He's our amazing Little Man, bringing joy and happiness to us all.

NONNA MARIA

and the Case of the Stolen Necklace

1.

SHE WAS FOUND with her back against the side of a pine tree. Dust and scattered cones nestled along the backs of her folded legs, thick strands of dark hair partially covering her face. One of her arms was leaning against the base of the tree and the other was laid out flat, fingers resting on the edge of the curved road. She was motionless, her eyes closed, her lips slightly parted. A gentle wind ruffled her blue-flowered dress, and one of her high-heeled shoes hung loose off her right foot.

It was seven in the morning on what would be another brutally hot summer day in Ischia, the sun rising above the calm waters of the port several miles below, its angled rays slowly beginning to wrap the woman in a blanket of warmth.

Two carabinieri officers parked their motorcycles at an angle to block off access to the road, patiently waiting for the medical examiner to arrive before allowing the body to be removed. A small group had gathered across the way—men and women who had been preparing to open their shops or head to work, stopped by the sight of the body of a woman none seemed to recognize.

The younger of the officers stared at the body, a concerned

look on his boyish face. "There's no blood anywhere," he said in a low voice. "It's almost as if she fell over and went to sleep."

"A sleep that lasts forever," the other officer said, stepping next to the young carabiniere. "Most likely a heart attack did her in. From the looks of it, she's been here a few hours. That puts the time of death in the middle of the night. Where would she be going? There's nothing around here at that hour but shuttered shops and a gas station. Closest house is at least a mile down the road."

A carabinieri car came up behind them, braking to a stop in front of the two motorcycles. The two officers turned from the woman's body and waited for their captain to approach them.

Captain Paolo Murino nodded at them and gave a quick glance at the group on the far side of the road. He stepped closer to the dead woman, his eyes taking in the curled body and the area where she had come to rest. "Who called it in?" he asked, without turning his head.

"Local fruit peddler," the younger officer said. "Told me he was driving past on his way down from his farm, his truck packed with deliveries."

"Did he stop to check on her?" Captain Murino asked.

"No, sir," the officer said. "He gave her only a passing look, thought she might have had too much to drink and fell asleep. And he was running late as it was."

"Did he leave you with a name?"

The younger carabiniere pulled a notebook from his jacket pocket and flipped open several pages. "Caldani," he said. "Bernardo Caldani."

"Check him out, make sure he is what he says he is," Murino said, staring at the younger of the two. "Your first week in Ischia, Franco, and you get to work a homicide. I'm certain that's not what you expected when you were transferred from Rome. Like anyone else who does a tour on the island, you were looking forward to days filled with quiet street patrols and flirting with tourists."

"What makes you so certain it was a homicide?" the second officer asked.

"Well, for one thing, her body would be at rest at that angle only if she had a number of broken bones," Captain Murino said. "I'm sure even you took note of that, Enrico."

"Yes, sir, I did," Enrico said. "But she could have fallen, tripped, and landed hard enough to break a bone or two."

"Perhaps," Captain Murino said, moving away from the two officers and standing in the center of the road. "But those two black skid marks tell me otherwise. If you compare them to the others on the road, you'll notice they are darker and deeper. That tells me they're fresh skid marks. Which might mean the woman's body was dumped or tossed from a car. She hit the ground hard, causing additional damage to her body."

"She is someone without a name," Franco said. "We didn't want to touch the body until the medical examiner signed off, but we looked for a bag or a purse and there wasn't any to be found."

"She has a name," Captain Murino said. "We just don't know it yet."

He turned to gaze out at the harbor below, where the first of the morning tourist boats were starting to head out for their trip around the island, and a packed hydrofoil was coming in to drop off another batch of guests. It was the second week of July and the tourists had been arriving in numbers far greater than any previous year. Murino had been stationed in Ischia for six years now and was still surprised by the thousands who flocked to the island each season. Ischia, eighteen miles off the Naples coast, had been, since the late 1960s, a prime vacation destination for a devoted number of Northern Italian, German, British, and American tourists who packed its many restaurants and beaches and enjoyed the supposedly healing powers of the thermal spas spread across the large island.

Captain Murino was in his mid-thirties, slim, with light brown razor-cut hair and, when the occasion called for it, a warm and engaging smile. He was engaged to a local girl he had planned to marry the previous fall. The wedding had been postponed, however, due to a family illness. It was now set for the following fall, weeks after the last of the tourists had left the island, and he planned to make Ischia his permanent home, providing his superiors didn't have another transfer in mind. He was a Northern Italian who had grown to love the island and its many customs and traditions, but was still regarded with suspicion by many of the locals. Over time, he was ever so slowly building up goodwill and trust among people who gave out such feelings with great reluctance.

"Canvass the area, talk to as many of the locals as you can," he said to the two officers. "Focus on the ones who live close by. Maybe one or two heard something or, with luck, saw something. Perhaps they might have a clue as to who this woman is or where she came from."

"Not exactly a pleasant way to begin a new day," Enrico said, looking back at the crowd, grown larger since he had first come onto the scene.

Captain Murino looked at Enrico for a moment and then turned and stared at the body of the dead woman lying on the side of the quiet road. "Or to end one," he said in a low voice.

2.

NONNA MARIA STOOD in front of the glass butcher's counter in
the open-air market of the port. It was early morning and the
large space was already filled with shoppers, mostly locals buying what they needed for the afternoon meal and a handful of
tourists who wandered through more out of curiosity than need.
Behind the counter, a tall young man was running a thick slab of
prosciutto through the slicing machine.

"I like it thin, Rafael," Nonna Maria said to the young man.
"But not so thin that the slices stick to the paper. That happened
to me last time I was here. Took more time to free the slices than
it did to make the panini."

"It's not my fault, Nonna Maria," Rafael said with a smile.
"This machine has a mind of its own. It cuts the way it wants
to cut."

"Then you should put the machine aside and cut the slices
with a knife," Nonna Maria said. "The way your father used to
do. He had a surgeon's touch."

"It was easier for him to pay attention to his work," Rafael
said, gazing around the crowded market. "There were fewer
distractions back when he stood behind this counter."

"Your father didn't have time for distractions," Nonna Maria said. "He had a family to feed and a business to run. You'll understand one day. Once you're married and have children of your own."

"He was never happier than when he was behind this counter," Rafael said. "He didn't think of it as a job. It was more like he was spending his days in the company of his friends."

"We felt the same way about him," Nonna Maria said. "It was a different island in those years. It's a much richer place now, our summers filled with tourists eager to spend money. And that makes it easier for our young men and women to earn a good living. But I miss those quiet days more and more. I suppose it is all part of getting old. But it's nice to keep memories of friends alive. Friends like your father."

"He said you were the one who talked him out of opening a restaurant and into setting up a butcher shop instead," Rafael said.

"It was more my husband, Gabriel, than me," Nonna Maria said. "But I agreed. Fabrizio hated crowds, and if a restaurant isn't crowded it goes out of business. But he loved talking to people and was a great salesman. And he made a success out of being a butcher. He worked hard and I never once saw him without a smile on his face."

Rafael wrapped the prosciutto in brown paper and taped it down on both ends. "I know you asked for a kilo," he said to Nonna Maria. "But I gave you a kilo and a half."

"Only if you let me pay for it," Nonna Maria said.

Rafael stepped out from behind the counter and rested a hand on Nonna Maria's shoulder. "Think of it as a gift," he said. "Not from me. From my father."

Nonna Maria smiled and nodded. "In that case, I thank you both," she said. "You for the kind gesture and your father for the delicious gift."

3.

ARIANNA CONTE RAN out of room 226 of the Grand Hotel Excelsior and bounded down two flights of stairs, bumping her hip against the curled iron railing just before reaching the entryway. She made a sharp left turn and came to a full stop at the front desk and slammed both her hands on the counter. She was short of breath, and a thin sheen of sweat coated her face and arms.

"I need to speak to the manager," she said, her loud voice echoing throughout the lobby. "And I need to speak to him now."

"He's on a long-distance call at the moment," the young woman behind the counter said, speaking in a mellow voice, looking to calm an agitated guest. "Is there anything I can do to help?"

"You can go inside and tell him to hang up on that call and get out here," Arianna Conte said, in an even louder voice. "And then you can put in a call to the police and have them here as soon as possible."

"The police?" the young woman said. "Why do you want me to call the police?"

"Why?" Arianna shouted. "I'll tell you why. My necklace

was stolen from out of my room! A very valuable necklace, one that has been in my family for generations, handed down to me by my own mother."

"Are you sure you didn't misplace it?" the young woman behind the counter asked.

Arianna stared at the girl for a few moments, her anger rising with each passing second. She read the name on the tag pinned to the young woman's white blouse. "I do not misplace anything, Branka," she said. "Especially something as valuable as that necklace. Now, do as I asked you to do. Get the manager and call the police. That woman needs to be arrested before she has a chance to leave the hotel."

"What woman?"

"What do you mean 'what woman'?" Arianna said, slamming a fist on the counter. "The one who stole my necklace. A member of your cleaning crew. She's been sniffing after that necklace since I checked in earlier this week. I had my suspicions about her, but I kept them to myself. If I had only acted sooner, none of this would have occurred."

"Did you see her take it?" Branka asked.

"I didn't have to witness it to know she's the one who stole it," Arianna said. "She's in my room morning, afternoon, and night. Waits until I leave for a meal or head to the beach. Always watching. And when I return, my things have always been moved, never in the places where I left them. Including my necklace, there, in plain sight, for her to see and to take."

"Why did you not make use of the safe in your room?" Branka asked.

"A child could break open that safe," Arianna said. "I've been in many five-star hotels in my travels and have never kept anything in any safe. That's the first place a thief looks when he, or in this case she, is looking to steal."

The hotel manager opened the door behind Branka and quietly stepped up to the counter. He was thin, of average height, with salt-and-pepper hair cropped short. He was wearing a crisp white shirt, open at the collar, and he stood directly across from Arianna. "I couldn't help but overhear," he said in a soothing voice. "The door to the office is not thick, as you can see."

"Then you are well aware that my precious necklace was stolen," Arianna said.

"I am well aware that you claim your necklace is missing," the hotel manager said. "But I assure you, we will not rest until it is found."

"She says someone on the cleaning staff has taken it," Branka said.

"So I understand," the hotel manager said. "Do you know the name of the alleged thief? You've said you've seen her multiple times, so I would imagine you got a look at her name tag, just as you are now looking at mine."

"Yes, Antonio," Arianna said. "I can describe her *and* name her. For you and for the police. Her name is Loretta, a petite young woman, always with an annoying smile on her face."

Antonio stood quietly for a few moments, looking at Arianna, her multicolored robe no doubt costing more than he earned in a month, thick curls of blond hair hanging down the sides of her face. She was in her mid-sixties, he guessed, and looked it, despite the daily herbal treatments meant to give her a more youthful appearance. This was her first stay at his hotel, unlike many of the other guests who returned season after season, making the Excelsior their yearly retreat.

"And you have no doubt it was Loretta who stole your necklace?" Antonio asked.

"None whatsoever," Arianna said.

"I heard you tell Branka the necklace has been in your family for generations," Antonio said. "I assume, then, that it's not an inexpensive piece of jewelry."

Arianna leaned in closer to the counter, inches from Antonio, and spoke in a lower voice, tinged with underlying rage. "It is worth more than the meager amount you and your staff could earn in a lifetime," she said.

Antonio nodded and turned to Branka. "Please put in a call to the carabinieri," he said to her. "Tell them we have a guest who wishes to report a theft. And then send one of the bellboys to go find Nonna Maria and ask her to come here as soon as she can."

"Why Nonna Maria?" Branka asked.

Antonio turned to face Arianna and smiled. "For many reasons," he said to Branka. "Prime among them is that Loretta is Nonna Maria's goddaughter. Which means this incident will be of great interest to her."

"Who is this Nonna Maria?" Arianna asked, not bothering to hide her frustration.

"If there has indeed been a theft," Antonio said, "she will be a great help to the police in finding the thief and returning the necklace to you."

"Is she a police officer?" Arianna asked.

Antonio shook his head. "No, Nonna Maria is not a member of the carabinieri," he said.

"What is she, then?"

"Nonna Maria is simply a friend," Antonio said. "A very good friend."

4.

NONNA MARIA WAS sitting on a stone bench in front of Saint Peter's Church. She was dressed in widow's black, the color she had worn every day since the death of her beloved husband, Gabriel, more than twenty years ago. She enjoyed watching the tourists parade past on the Corso Vittoria Colonna, heading off to the numerous pristine beaches or the many spas dotting Ischia during the day and, come sundown, dressed in their finest summer outfits eager to enjoy a meal in one of the popular restaurants that were always filled to capacity this time of year.

Nonna Maria was in her seventies, though there were only a select few, besides her grown children and childhood friends, who knew her real age. She was short, walked with a slight limp favoring her right hip, and had a thick head of hair, white as a cloud, held together in a bun by an array of black pins. She was known and trusted by the island locals and had, over the course of many years, been the one they turned to if they needed help or advice. She was the one they went to see to help settle a family dispute or bring an end to a long-festering feud between neighbors. She was always there to offer financial advice, and sometimes aid, to those hampered by such problems. And, on a number of occasions, Nonna Maria had been called on to help a friend out of a much more serious problem, either accused of committing a crime or being involved in one.

She had no training in these matters, nor did she claim to possess the skills of a seasoned detective. What Nonna Maria did have was a wide network of contacts throughout the island and as far away as Rome (though she had never set foot in that city). And she had the trust of the people of Ischia, earned through years of friendship and loyalty. She could be counted on to keep her word and never betray a trust. She didn't bother with idle gossip, and when not off helping a friend in need, she was content to drink more than her share of coffee during the day and white wine in the evening and cook large, flavorful meals for her family. She doted on her many grand- and great-grandchildren and loved to sit at her dining room table, listening to the Neapolitan love ballads sung by her next-door neighbor.

Nonna Maria thought of herself as a simple woman living a simple life in the only place she had ever called home. She had lived in her two-story stone house for over fifty years now and could never imagine herself anywhere else. It was the home she and her husband had bought when they first married, where she had raised a family, enjoyed moments of great happiness, and suffered through the grief of numerous tragedies. Through the years, she had seen friends and relatives age and prosper as the island grew in popularity. She had also seen far too many loved ones die from either accident or illness, often brought down at much too young an age.

She was not an educated woman and never read a newspaper or magazine or book. She had not been to a movie or the theater in her life. Yet, despite that, Nonna Maria was intuitively smart and had a keen eye for observation. "A friend comes to her with a problem and she knows what steps need to be taken to help work it out," Sophia Ventura, an old family friend, used to tell those who marveled at Nonna Maria's ability to solve both disputes and criminal matters. "And she has eyes and ears everywhere. In that sense, Nonna Maria is a detective. The best one we have on Ischia."

She worked closely with the captain of the carabinieri, Paolo Murino, and over the past six years, a mutual respect and friendship had taken root. Nonna Maria never took credit for helping to solve a case. And she did her best not to interfere in police matters. As she often said, all she ever set out to do was offer help to a friend in need.

That was her one mission and her true calling. And on an island populated by 65,000 and crammed with an additional half a million seasonal visitors, there was no better friend to have than Nonna Maria.

5.

FEDERICO CASTAGNA SPOTTED Nonna Maria from across the crowded Corso and made his way toward the stone bench where she was sitting. She smiled at him as soon as she saw him approach, waving to her as he did. "I've been looking for you all morning," he said, bending down and kissing her on both cheeks.

"And now you've found me," Nonna Maria said.

"Would you mind if I sat down?" he asked.

"It's not my bench, Federico," Nonna Maria said. "So, please, sit and tell me why you look so agitated."

Federico Castagna was a frail young man in his late twenties, his brown hair already beginning to thin at the top and his thick-framed eyeglasses seeming always in need of a proper cleaning. Nonna Maria had known him since he was a child. He had been a sad boy who had witnessed a number of tragedies at much too young an age. His father died when Federico was eight, one of several victims of a train derailment fifty miles outside Naples. His mother had suffered a stroke when Federico was still in his teens and he helped care for her and his younger sister, Isabella, while attending school and working part-time in a pastry shop near his small apartment on Via Casciaro. He was a good student and had applied himself to his schoolwork and now had a solid position as a junior accountant with a firm that handled the funds for a number of the island's businesses.

Despite what he had accomplished and his loving devotion to his mother and sister, there was a sadness he carried around like a weight. He had few friends on the island, stayed to himself, and was shy when approached. He seemed to live a life filled with darkness on an island drenched in sunshine.

Federico sat next to Nonna Maria and wiped his brow with a handful of loose tissues. "There was an incident last night," he said, speaking in a low tone, each word measured. "Just outside of Barano. The police are starting to look into it. So, at this point, I can't say for certain whether what happened was an accident or a murder."

"How do you know all this?" Nonna Maria asked. "Were you there, or are you passing on what you've been told?"

Federico stayed silent for a moment, tissues balled up in his hands. He was nervous and glanced at the faces of the tourists and locals as they passed in front of the church. "I was there," he finally said. "I had driven up to have dinner with my sister and her family and was on my way back to my apartment. I stayed longer than I had planned and, as you know, the roads down from Barano are not lit late at night."

"The sharp turns and curves make driving even more difficult," Nonna Maria said. "But you know enough to go slowly and not to have too much wine with your meal before having to go out on the road."

"I didn't drink at all, Nonna Maria," Federico said. "And I

was going slowly, taking each curve as gently as I could manage. But the fog was heavy last night and it was difficult keeping my windshield clear. And my vision, even with these glasses, isn't the best."

Nonna Maria leaned closer and reached for Federico's hands, holding them softly. The young man was shaking and clearly frightened. She could see his body tremble and he had a hard time catching his breath.

"What are you trying to tell me, Federico?" Nonna Maria asked. "Were you involved in this incident?"

Federico shook his head and squeezed Nonna Maria's hands. "I came around a bend, it was a tight turn and caught me by surprise. I felt a bump against the front of my car, on the right side, and heard a loud noise. I stopped soon as I could, on the other side of the curve, and I got out."

"Did you see anything or anyone?" Nonna Maria asked.

"It was too dark to see," he said. "All the shops were closed and the blinds drawn on the apartments above them. I walked up several feet and didn't see anything. I thought maybe I had run over some poor animal or hit a barrier of some kind. And the evening fog was so thick it was difficult to see more than ten feet ahead of me. After a few minutes, I walked back to my car and drove home."

"So, it wasn't until this morning that you heard about this incident?" Nonna Maria asked. "When your sister called you?"

Federico nodded. "How did you know it was my sister who called?"

"Because I know she's the kind of sister who would want to make sure you made it home safely and to make sure you enjoyed the evening spent in the company of her family," Nonna Maria said. "It's what any sister would do."

"She called as I was about to leave my apartment and head to the office," Federico said. "At first, she told me how much my niece and nephew enjoyed seeing me and that we should plan on another dinner later this month. And then she told me a woman had been found dead by the side of a road leading down to the port. She said the area was flooded with carabinieri and municipal police going door-to-door asking if anyone had seen or heard anything during the night. And that's when I thought back to that moment with my car. When I thought I had hit something, or maybe someone."

"Did your sister tell you the name of the person that was hit near her home?" Nonna Maria asked.

Federico stared at Nonna Maria, his eyes glistened with tears, streaming down both sides of his face. "I don't have a name and I don't think the police do, either. All I know is it was a woman, Nonna Maria, and her body was found early this morning. Found very close to where I drove past last night."

"And you think you might have hit her with your car?" Nonna Maria asked.

Federico nodded. "A woman is dead, Nonna Maria," he managed to say in between sobs. "And I may well have been the one who killed her."

"Compose yourself, Federico," Nonna Maria said. "Go to your office and focus on your work. It's all you can do for now."

"The police will want to talk to me," Federico said. "It's only a matter of time before they find out I drove past the area where the body was found."

"I know," Nonna Maria said. "And when they come, you simply tell them the truth. Which is what I know you will do."

"And what will you do, Nonna Maria?" Federico asked.

Nonna Maria stood and rested a hand on one side of Federico's face. "What I have always tried to do," Nonna Maria said. "Help my friends when they need me."

6.

NONNA MARIA WALKED past the two carabinieri officers stationed in front of the open gates leading to the garden-lined entrance of the Grand Hotel Excelsior. A taxi-van was parked by the entrance, the driver leaning against one of the sliding passenger doors. He was middle-aged, balding, with a handsome face and an expressive manner on most days. Today was not one of those days.

He looked up when he saw Nonna Maria and waved in her direction. She walked over to his van. "You look troubled, Giovanni," Nonna Maria said. "It seems to be the day for it."

"I am heartbroken, Nonna Maria," Giovanni said.

"You're not the only one," Nonna Maria said. "It's not even time for lunch and there's already a great deal of trouble on the island."

"You heard, then, about the woman found on the road near Barano?" Giovanni said.

Nonna Maria nodded. "And a bellboy from the hotel caught up with me on Via Roma and told me my goddaughter has been accused of stealing a necklace from one of the hotel's guests," she said. "And now I see you with a sad look on your face and a heavy heart to go with it."

"Do you remember when one of my cats was run over by a hit-and-run driver last winter?" he asked. "And you offered to help find the driver who did it?"

Nonna Maria nodded. "I wasn't the only one who helped," she said. "You have many good friends, Giovanni. And you have rescued so many stray cats and dogs over the years, not even Saint Francis could keep up with you."

"I called the local police and the carabinieri three times to report the incident, but no one ever came," Giovanni said. "A dead cat wasn't important enough for them to come investigate. But as soon as someone with money calls, or even just someone they think has money, look how fast they come running."

"Even without their help, the driver was found," Nonna Maria said. "And he was fined for driving with an expired license."

"And the lawyer you helped me find proved he had been drinking. He went before a magistrate and ended up serving a three-month sentence in a Naples jail," Giovanni said.

"Justice can be served in many ways," Nonna Maria said. "What matters is he was caught, not who did the catching."

"And now instead of one of my cats, it's a poor young woman who is dead on the side of the road," Giovanni said.

"Did you know this woman?" Nonna Maria asked.

Giovanni shook his head. "It just makes me sad to hear such things," he said. "This is such a beautiful island, Nonna Maria, filled with fine people and thousands of tourists during the season. Yet, every summer, it seems we are faced with one tragedy after another."

"It's a sad part of life, Giovanni," Nonna Maria said. "Just because we are lucky to call Ischia our home doesn't free us from dangers."

"I won't keep you any longer, Nonna Maria," Giovanni said. "And if you should need any help with whatever is going on in there, you know where to find me."

"How many dogs and cats do you have now on your farm?" Nonna Maria asked.

"At last count, there were twenty-seven," Giovanni said with a smile. "Each one happy and content. They love roaming the property, and most of all, they love my wife's cooking."

"I changed my mind. You are not the saint, Giovanni," Nonna Maria said. "Your wife is the one who should have a statue in her name."

7.

NONNA MARIA MOVED slowly across the stone pathway leading to the doors of the Excelsior. Branka was behind the counter and gave Nonna Maria a warm smile. Branka had known Nonna Maria since she was a child newly arrived with her parents from Croatia. Nonna Maria had found her family an apartment in the port area and helped ease their transition to life on an island not accustomed to strangers. "I knew you would be here soon as you heard," she said. "Loretta is on the second floor, talking to one of the carabinieri."

"How is she?" Nonna Maria asked.

"I only got a quick glimpse of her, but she seems to be holding up," Branka said. "I would imagine she's upset, and if I were in her place, a bit angry. To be charged with a crime, any crime, is enough to shock anyone."

"Accused," Antonio said, stepping out of his office and up to the counter. "Not yet charged."

"Are there any other witnesses to Loretta's crime?" Nonna Maria asked. "Other than the woman who says her necklace was stolen?"

"None as yet, Nonna Maria," Antonio said. "But it's still very early in the investigation."

"So, what happens to Loretta while the carabinieri go about their business?" Nonna Maria asked.

Antonio drew a deep breath before he answered. "She's been relieved of her post," he said. "She is no longer a member of the staff."

"Without knowing for sure that she actually took this necklace?" Nonna Maria said.

"I'm afraid so, Nonna Maria," Antonio said. "I had no other choice."

"There is always a choice, Antonio," Nonna Maria said.

"I realize she's your goddaughter," Antonio said. "But I have a responsibility to the hotel and to the guests who stay here. And given that we're in the middle of the summer season, I need to find a replacement for her as soon as possible. I know you don't agree with me on this, Nonna Maria. But it was a decision that had to be made."

"Do you believe Loretta took this woman's necklace?" Nonna Maria asked.

"It doesn't matter what I believe, Nonna Maria," Antonio said. "While she stands accused, she cannot be allowed to work in this hotel. It would not be right. The guests would be uncomfortable, as would some members of the staff. Those feelings must come before any others."

"Loretta loved working here," Nonna Maria said. "It was a fresh start for her, especially given her difficulties in the past. Difficulties I made you aware of when I recommended her to you. She had found a new path and was the happiest I had seen her in a long time."

"That was true until this morning, Nonna Maria," Antonio said. "Until she stood accused of stealing an expensive necklace from one of my guests. That accusation changed her standing with me and with the hotel owners. I did what needed to be done."

Nonna Maria nodded. "And I will do the same," she said.

She turned away from the counter and walked toward the hotel's large salon, a large black tote bag flung over her right shoulder.

8.

NONNA MARIA SAT across from Captain Murino on the sun-drenched terrace overlooking the thermal pool. They watched a middle-aged woman do a series of laps, while around her sat a half-dozen guests in lounge chairs covered with beach towels, reading books and enjoying the morning warmth.

"Where is the woman who accused Loretta of taking the necklace?" she asked.

"In the dining room waiting to talk to me," Captain Murino said. "You can join us if you like."

"What do you know about her?" Nonna Maria said. "Other than she says her necklace is missing and claims my goddaughter is the one who took it."

"One of my officers spoke to her at length earlier," Captain Murino said. "This is her first visit to Ischia and, based on the circumstances, likely her last. She's from Turin, is here alone, and spends her time traveling throughout Europe."

"How much does she say the necklace is worth?" Nonna Maria asked.

"She claims it's priceless," Captain Murino said, "and cannot be replaced. It has been in the family for generations and there are decades of memories attached to its worth."

"Did your officer believe her?"

"It's not his place to offer an opinion," Captain Murino said. "He is there to gather facts, nothing more."

"Lies can always be presented as facts, Captain," Nonna Maria said. "And if told well, they are easier to believe. The truth is much more difficult to uncover."

"You have a personal stake in this, Nonna Maria," Captain Murino said. "The woman has charged your goddaughter with the theft. And while I know you don't believe Loretta capable of committing such an act, she does stand accused."

"I never interfere with your work, Captain," Nonna Maria said. "As you are well aware. But I will look into the matter on behalf of my goddaughter. In my own way, of course."

"The owner of the necklace, Arianna Conte, claims your goddaughter was in her room three times a day," Captain Murino said. "Early morning, late afternoon, and in the evening. The necklace was always left on the glass countertop of a bureau in the area just off the main room."

"Loretta would not be doing her job if she were not in the woman's room during those times," Nonna Maria said. "She helps clean the room in the morning, brings a fresh bottle of water, fruit, and clean laundry in the afternoon, and prepares the room for the evening. At least that's what Loretta told me her duties were when Antonio hired her at the start of the season."

"That part is true," Captain Murino admitted.

"What part isn't?" Nonna Maria asked.

"Signora Conte claims the room was never found as she had left it," Captain Murino said. "Items were moved from one place to another, even her clothing was rearranged every time she returned to her room."

"Sheets need to be changed," Nonna Maria said. "A bed needs to be made. If there is a dress or a blouse on the bed, it would need to be moved in order for the task to be completed."

Captain Murino nodded. "Signora Conte isn't accusing anyone of taking any clothing," he said. "Only her necklace."

"Has anyone besides Signora Conte seen this necklace?" Nonna Maria asked. "Members of the hotel staff or some of the other guests dining at the restaurant?"

"Not that I'm aware," Captain Murino said. "But we have only just begun our investigation. What are you getting at, Nonna Maria?"

"If this necklace is as valuable as Signora Conte says, then why not wear it to dinner to allow others to admire it?" Nonna Maria said. "And if she had no plans to wear it at all, then why bother bringing it on her trip?"

"Questions yet to be asked, Nonna Maria," Captain Murino said, "and worthy of an answer. In the meantime, tell me a bit about Loretta."

"Has she been arrested?" Nonna Maria asked.

"She's been placed under house arrest," Captain Murino said. "Until we have gathered more information. Her mother has assured me she will abide by the order that Loretta not leave the premises without permission from my office. For the moment, she remains our primary suspect."

"A primary suspect without a job," Nonna Maria said.

"Antonio had little choice in the matter," Captain Murino said. "He cannot have a member of his staff accused of a crime and do nothing. You would do the same if you were in his position, Nonna Maria."

"I would never want to be in a position where I would need to have someone fired on the word of a stranger," Nonna Maria said.

"I understand how you feel," Captain Murino said. "But the harsh reality is if Antonio had not acted as he did, then he would have been replaced by the hotel owners."

"What if the necklace is not found?" Nonna Maria asked. "What happens then?"

"It will come down to her word against that of Signora Conte," Captain Murino said.

Nonna Maria took a folded white handkerchief from the pocket of her black dress and wiped a line of sweat from her upper lip.

"Let's move to the sitting area in the foyer," Captain Murino said. "It's much cooler there. "

Captain Murino stood and they walked together from the patio, past the double glass doors, to a massive room filled with plush chairs and comfortable couches. The morning papers were spread out on a trio of glass coffee tables and an array of fresh-cut flowers filled a half-dozen large vases resting in nooks, on counters, and atop a grand piano. Nonna Maria sat in one of the chairs and Captain Murino leaned back against the soft fabric of a two-seat couch across from her.

"I would offer to have the staff bring you a coffee, but I know you well enough to realize it would be a wasted request," Captain Murino said.

"No need to trouble anyone," Nonna Maria said. "I have a

fresh pot waiting for me in my kitchen. The only coffee I have ever tasted was made on that stove."

"You might surprise yourself," Captain Murino said. "You might enjoy drinking a coffee made by hands other than your own."

"I'm too old for surprises," Nonna Maria said.

"On to Loretta, then," Captain Murino said.

"My friend Concetta was widowed twenty years back, around the same time my husband died," Nonna Maria said. There was sadness in her voice on those rare occasions when she talked about her Gabriel and his death. "We were close prior to that sad time, but the loss of our husbands brought us even closer."

"I wasn't aware I was dredging up sad memories, Nonna Maria," Captain Murino said. "I apologize for that."

"You asked about Loretta," Nonna Maria said. "And in order to know her, you need to know her story. And you've been on Ischia long enough to know, Captain, that the people here cherish their memories, both the happy and the sad. I am no different."

"That's true everywhere, Nonna Maria," Captain Murino said. "Not just here in Ischia."

"I imagine so," Nonna Maria said.

"So, Loretta must have been barely out of diapers when her father died," Captain Murino said. "The manager, Antonio, showed me her work application. She's not yet twenty-two years old."

"My husband and I were blessed with many children," Nonna Maria said. "But Concetta and her husband, Bruno, did not have any. As the weeks went by after Bruno's death, Concetta's days grew long and lonely. It was then that I placed a call to the girl's orphanage in Pompeii. I asked the Mother Superior if a widow would be allowed to adopt one of the infants as her own."

"A Mother Superior whom you had helped out on more than one occasion," Captain Murino said.

"That part of the story must remain between myself and the good Mother," Nonna Maria said. "I was told it was possible for a widow to adopt, especially since Concetta owned a successful grocery store and had the means to care for a child."

"And Concetta raised the child as her own," Captain Murino said. "Did she remarry?"

"She had already had a husband, one she loved," Nonna Maria said. "There was no room in her heart for another. But there was plenty there for a child, and Concetta and Loretta are as close as any mother and daughter can be."

"Was she ever in any trouble?"

"Loretta has a hot temper, that is well known," Nonna Maria said. "And there were a few fights with other children in the years she was at school. It wasn't a secret she was adopted and had previously been abandoned as an infant on a street corner in Naples. Some of the other students teased her, and Loretta was not one to let an insult go unanswered."

"Did she fall in with a bad crowd?" Captain Murino asked. "Very often, kids in her circumstances find it easier to be accepted by the ones already looking for trouble. It's only natural."

"She didn't spend her free time with the best students in her class," Nonna Maria said. "But she didn't go looking to cause trouble."

"So, never any problems with the law?" Captain Murino asked. "Until now, that is."

"If there had been, you would already have heard about it," Nonna Maria said. "No one is claiming Loretta was a perfect child, she had her wild side and she got into her share of scrapes, but nothing that would be brought to your attention."

"She was suspended from school on more than one occasion," Captain Murino said. "Due to these scrapes that sometimes occurred."

"She's long since moved past those days," Nonna Maria said. "She's now a grown woman and a hardworking one, caring and affectionate, and very loyal to her mother. She would do nothing to bring her embarrassment or shame."

"I would not expect you to believe Loretta capable of stealing anything," Captain Murino said. "Much less a valuable necklace from a hotel room."

"Not just any hotel, Captain," Nonna Maria said. "But the hotel where she works. She would be a fool to commit a crime here, and yes, Loretta may have a temper, but she is no fool. Ask yourself this, Captain: What would be the point of her stealing such a necklace? She couldn't wear it or sell it or give it as a gift. If she did any of those things, many on the island would notice and grow suspicious as to how she acquired such an expensive piece. Questions would be asked and answers would be difficult to come by. So, why even bother taking it?"

"The necklace could have caught her eye and she took it without thinking through the consequences," Captain Murino said. "Many thefts are simply an act of impulse rather than intent."

Nonna Maria glanced up at the large painting hanging on the wall above the couch, lost in thought for several moments. "You now know a bit about Loretta," she said, looking back at Captain Murino. "Now it's time to look at the other side of the coin."

"Which is?"

"What do you know about Signora Arianna Conte?" Nonna Maria asked.

9.

THE GARDEN RESTAURANT was empty, the dozen or so tables dressed for the evening crowd. Nonna Maria sat and gazed out at the tables, shaded by plants of various sizes, low-hanging trees, and potted plants filled with an assortment of fruits and vegetables. Magnums of red wine were placed against low stone walls and fresh bottles of mineral water rested on each table. In the distance, through the mist and floating clouds, she could make out the sea and the island of Procida, a half-hour boat ride from her beloved Ischia.

It was early afternoon and most of the island was at rest, taking a break from a morning spent in the sun and a long midday meal. She watched as Gennaro Rossi, her friend of many decades, poured himself a cool glass of his homemade white wine, his fourth of the day. He tilted the bottle toward the empty glass next to Nonna Maria's right elbow. "I know it's early for you," he said, "but what harm can a half glass of my wine do?"

"Homemade wine makes my eyes heavy," Nonna Maria said. "And yours is twice as strong as any on the island. It's the perfect cure for people who have trouble sleeping."

Gennaro slapped the wooden table with a beefy hand and laughed, the sound echoing through the valley surrounding them. He was a large, heavyset man with a thick mane of brown hair and a salt-and-pepper beard in serious need of a trim. He was born in Ischia, left as a young man in search of riches and adventures, and experienced both during his forty years traveling the country and the world. He returned to Ischia a married man with a wife and two grown daughters. He settled into the small house on the five-acre parcel of land left to him by his father and was initially content to plant his fruits and vegetables and sell them at a small profit. Two seasons of little income forced him to change course and he turned his home into a restaurant, making meals from what he grew on his property. In a short time, his home became one of the most popular restaurants on the island, a destination for tourists and locals alike.

"Since you didn't come here to drink and I know you're not looking for a meal, there must be another reason for your visit to my garden," Gennaro said.

"Maybe I just wanted to sit and visit with an old friend I have not seen for too long a time," Nonna Maria said, resting her black tote bag on top of the table.

"I know you better than that, Nonna Maria," Gennaro said. "You're not a woman who likes to waste her time."

"That's because I'm old, Gennaro," Nonna Maria said. "I don't have much time left to waste."

He reached across the table and rested a large hand on top of one of Nonna Maria's gnarled ones and smiled at her. "You want to know what I know about the woman they found down the road," he said. "And what the talk among the locals is about her. Talk they keep among themselves and don't risk passing on to the carabinieri."

"Do they know who she is?" Nonna Maria asked.

"I haven't heard a name yet," Gennaro said. "From what little I could pick up, she doesn't appear to be a tourist, but at the same time, no one seems to know her. If she's a local, she's been away for quite a while and doesn't seem to have family on the island."

"You were away for forty years, if not more, and you still have family on the island," Nonna Maria said. "It's hard to be a local and not be connected to someone by blood."

"I agree," Gennaro said. "It is a confusing puzzle. You can throw a rock into a crowd on Ischia and you're bound to hit two or three cousins. And at least one of them will owe you money."

"Why are the carabinieri so certain she is not a tourist?" Nonna Maria asked.

"All the hotels were contacted," Gennaro said. "Not just the ones in the area but those throughout the island. Bed and breakfast places as well. No one reported an unaccounted-for guest."

"She could have been visiting for the day," Nonna Maria said. "Came here early in the morning and planned to leave after dinner."

"Yet she didn't," Gennaro said. "The last hydrofoil leaves port at eleven-thirty, the Lauro boat pulls out at midnight. That's more than enough time on the island for a day-tripper."

Nonna Maria was silent for a few moments, content to gaze out at the expansive view and allow her thoughts to roam. "Do they know how she died?"

"If they do, I have yet to hear it," Gennaro said. "But all you need to do is ask your friend Captain Murino. I doubt very much he would be reluctant to tell you."

"I haven't talked to him about this yet," Nonna Maria. "Not until I know for sure who she is and how she died."

"That's not like you, Nonna Maria," Gennaro said. "Captain Murino is your trusted friend. What is it that concerns you so much you can't talk to him about it?"

"A young man I know may be involved," Nonna Maria said. "He was driving on the road a few hours before the woman's body was found."

"The roads here are as dark as a cave," Gennaro said. "And the streets are empty after midnight, not even stray cats venture out. If your friend, by misfortune, ran into this woman, it would surely be ruled an accident."

Nonna Maria nodded. "The law may well see it that way," she said. "If that is what happened. But my friend would not. He would blame himself, and it would ruin the rest of his life."

"I will do anything you need me to do, Nonna Maria," Gennaro said. "Both for your friend and for your goddaughter, who I've been told is also now in harm's way."

"We have both lived long enough to know the world can be a dark place, Gennaro, even on an island as beautiful as Ischia," Nonna Maria said.

Nonna Maria pushed back her chair, stood, and picked up her large black tote bag. She gave Gennaro a warm embrace, then turned and walked slowly down the stone path, toward the rusty iron gate leading out of the safe confines of her friend's lush garden.

10.

LORETTA FABRINI STOOD against the cold stone wall of her apartment building, still wearing her work uniform, quietly facing an uncertain future. She was not yet twenty-two years old, petite, with long dark hair and an easy manner. She had been working at the Excelsior since the start of the season and enjoyed the work and had made friends with several of her co-workers. The hours were long, a twelve-hour shift beginning at seven in the morning, with a one-hour break for lunch between noon and one. But the seven hundred and fifty euros she earned per month, along with the tips that were shared by the household staff, gave her a feeling of independence she had not known before. It allowed her to contribute to the family expenses, put a small amount in savings, and still have enough left over to pay for her clothing and social activities.

She rode a bicycle to and from work and then would rush home and tell her mother about her day—sharing stories about the hotel's eclectic clientele, from the elderly man in room 118 who always wore a cream-colored suit to dinner each evening, to the two sisters from somewhere in Germany who would sit under the hot Ischia sun for hours at a time, determined to return home as tan as possible. There was the British man who carried a thick pencil and large drawing pad with him wherever he went and would often leave one of his sketches in his room for her with a note attached, and a charming Northern Italian couple who ate all their meals in their room, the husband too frail to endure long walks, both content to read and nap under the large open umbrellas on the terrace.

The long days and hard work were made easier by these encounters, and Loretta dreamed of one day owning a small hotel of her own and playing hostess to a variety of clients from different parts of the world. But her dreams were shattered earlier that morning when she was accused of stealing a necklace. Now she was filled with a feeling of dread, and for the first time in her young life, Loretta Fabrini was frightened, facing a future that could only bring ruin.

11.

NONNA MARIA WALKED past the Banco di Napoli and made her way toward Loretta's apartment building, her limp a bit more pronounced than normal this early evening. But this was not a time to be concerned about minor aches and pains. There was work to be done and solutions to be found, though a great deal was still unknown to her. But Nonna Maria had a wide network of friends and connections and knew she would need their help in guiding her to find the answers to both matters that needed to be resolved.

"I'm sorry I kept you waiting," Nonna Maria said to Loretta, standing now before the young woman and noticing the fear and apprehension in her eyes. "I stopped off to see one of my grandchildren, the youngest. He hurt himself in a fall the other day and I went to see how he was feeling."

"Is it serious?" Loretta asked.

"He's six and fell while climbing a tree in his backyard," Nonna Maria said. "It is what boys that age do. But he will be fine in a day or two. And it won't stop him from climbing trees. I brought him a box of almond biscotti, his favorite. That should keep him occupied for a while."

"I'm sorry to take you away from your family," Loretta said. "I don't know who else to talk to about this mess I'm in."

"You've taken me away from nothing," Nonna Maria said. "Walk with me back to my house while we talk. I prepared a meal for you. I know you haven't eaten all day, and no problem, either big or small, can ever be solved on an empty stomach."

"I'm under house arrest, Nonna Maria," Loretta said. "I can't go anywhere without permission from the carabinieri."

"I spoke to Captain Murino," Nonna Maria said. "I guaranteed him there would be no crimes committed while you had a meal at my house."

"I don't think I could eat anything," Loretta said. "My stomach is in knots."

"I have just the meal that will untie those knots," Nonna Maria said. "You'll start with a bowl of pasta with zucchini and then you'll move to a platter of lemon chicken, some fried peppers and capers and marinated artichokes. I have a few loaves of homemade olive bread and a jug of cold D'Ambra white wine with sliced peaches for later, along with some pastries from Minicucci's bar."

"It sounds wonderful," Loretta said, smiling for the first time that day. "I should let my mother know I won't be home for dinner."

"No need," Nonna Maria said. "I've sent word already. She knows you're with me and will return home after dinner, with the leftovers for both of you to enjoy."

They rounded the corner past Saint Peter's Church and began to walk down the sloping street toward Nonna Maria's home. It was a two-story stone house less than a quarter of a mile from the local beach, one that Nonna Maria had never once visited.

"How was it left with you and the carabinieri?" Nonna Maria asked.

"Two of the officers asked me a few questions," Loretta said. "And then I was told I was free to return home while they continued their investigation. Antonio, the manager, had already relieved me of my duties."

"Did you ever see this necklace?" Nonna Maria asked.

"Not that I remember," Loretta said. "The signora had quite a bit of jewelry lying about the room, but nothing like the necklace she described."

"How did the signora treat you and your co-workers?" Nonna Maria asked. "Was she friendly or distant?"

"She spoke to me a few times," Loretta said. "Never in a friendly tone. She would summon me into her room when she wanted to point something out."

"Like what?"

"It was always about an item that had been misplaced," Loretta said. "A watch under her bed one time, and a scarf behind the bathroom door another. She would always ask if I was the one who had put them there."

"Were you the only one on the cleaning staff she spoke to about these things?" Nonna Maria asked.

Loretta nodded. "I asked the others, and they had very little contact with her," she said. "But her room was assigned to me, so maybe that's the reason she came to me with her issues."

"But you didn't clean the room by yourself, right?"

"That's right," Loretta said. "Three of us would go in together. One to do the bed, change the sheets. Another to clean the bathrooms and replace the towels, and a third to mop the floors."

"And the two others who worked with you," Nonna Maria said, "did they happen to notice a necklace in the room?"

"No, Nonna Maria," Loretta said. "As far as I know, no one on the cleaning staff saw a necklace, large or small, in that room."

"And Antonio tells me it wasn't seen by anyone on the dining room staff," Nonna Maria said. "And there would be no reason for the signora to wear such a treasured family item to the beach or at the pool."

They reached the stairwell to Nonna Maria's house and stopped for a moment. "What do you think that all means, Nonna Maria?" Loretta asked.

"Little one, you have been accused of stealing a necklace that no one has seen," Nonna Maria said. "So, either it was left under an item of clothing or in a place no one else who entered the room would notice it, or we are dealing with an even bigger problem than a stolen necklace."

12.

ENRICO THE JEWELER stood behind the glass counter of his large store, a heavy plastic bag filled with jars of tomato sauce and marinated peppers resting near his left arm. He smiled at Nonna Maria. "You don't need to bring me something every time you come to my shop," he said to her in a gentle voice. "Your company is a gift all its own. You have brightened my morning more than the hot sun above us."

"You're doing me a favor," Nonna Maria said. "I made more sauce and peppers than I know what to do with. Some years turn out like that. And who better to benefit than an old and trusted friend?"

Enrico smiled and nodded his thanks, then lifted the bag and placed it under the counter. He was Ischia's premier jeweler, a short, bald man of even temperament, with an encyclopedic knowledge of anything having to do with diamonds, pearls, and gold. He was in his mid-sixties and had spent decades away from Ischia learning as much as he could of his chosen trade. He had tutored under the masters in Venice, Paris, and Florence, where he partnered with the legendary jeweler Fabrizio Carmellotto, working with him side by side in a shop on the Ponte Vecchio for a dozen years. He returned to the island seven years ago and opened his jewelry store on Via Roma soon after.

During the summer season, the store attracted more tourists than it did locals, since the items Enrico sold were on the high end and beyond the financial means of most of the working men and women who made Ischia their home. But in the winter months, long after the tourists had gone back to their lives and normal routines, Enrico would mark down many of the items in his shop by as much as sixty percent, enticing many locals to purchase rings, watches, necklaces, earrings, and bracelets they normally would not be able to afford.

Enrico slid open a panel under the glass counter and gently eased out a thin silver bracelet and placed it on a velvet strip. He looked up at Nonna Maria and smiled. "This is one of my favorites," he said to her. "And I would be more than happy to sell it to you for the price I paid for it. No profit for me. Only joy in knowing that a dear friend was wearing it."

"I'm not a good customer for you, Enrico," Nonna Maria said. "I dislike jewelry and flowers in equal measure. I've never worn anything other than my wedding band. That stays with me until I die."

Enrico nodded and moved the bracelet to one side of the counter. "I know," he said with a smile. "I was just checking to see if you had mellowed any since we last saw each other."

"I'm happy to see I didn't disappoint you," Nonna Maria said.

"But since, as I expected, you didn't come to buy, and I know you to be too busy just to stroll by for a visit, what is it that I can assist you with?" Enrico asked.

"There's a signora staying at the Excelsior," Nonna Maria said. "She claims to be very wealthy, coming from a rich and noble family in the North. At least that's what she has told the carabinieri and anyone else at the hotel close enough to hear her voice."

"This is the same signora who claims to have had a valuable necklace stolen from her room?" Enrico asked.

Nonna Maria nodded. "It's good to know Captain Murino also knows who to turn to for answers when it comes to jewelry," she said. "How much value did you put to the necklace?"

"It is hard to say without actually seeing it, holding it in my hands," Enrico said. "If it is in the condition the signora claims it is, and if it was made in Malta as she says, then it would be worth anywhere between three hundred and five hundred thousand euros. Not a necklace at the highest end, but still one of substantial value."

"The signora, Arianna Conte, says she was born and raised in Florence and was given the necklace by her mother while they both lived in that city," Nonna Maria said. "You spent many years there and your shop sold quite a bit of jewelry to those with the financial means to afford it. And you also were asked to have items appraised, to see if their value had increased down the years. At least, from what I've heard told."

"That's true, Nonna Maria," Enrico said. "The majority of our customers were either rich tourists or locals with deep pockets and a strong desire to own the finest jewelry their money could buy. Many of them looked upon their jewelry as investments, as one would look at a house or a vineyard. They would often come to us to see to what degree their possessions had increased in value."

"In your time there, did you do any business with a wealthy family named Conte?" Nonna Maria asked.

"Off the top of my head, I would say no," Enrico said. "I would need to go back and check my sales records, in the event my memory has failed me. But while there are many things I forget as I get older, I never forget the name of a good customer. But Conte is a common name in the North, so I would need to take a deeper look."

"As you may have heard, my goddaughter, Loretta, has been accused of stealing the necklace," Nonna Maria said.

"That's the word spread among those eager to spread the word," Enrico said.

"What could a young woman like Loretta do with such a necklace if she had taken it?" Nonna Maria asked.

"She would look to sell it to someone who knew how to move it on the black market," Enrico said. "She would be paid about one-third the worth of the necklace and would be forever clear of it."

"And who on Ischia has the money and connections to move a necklace off the island and onto the black market?" Nonna Maria asked.

"There are others on the island who sell jewelry, but they are mostly locals moving lower-end cuts and less expensive items to tourists looking for gifts to bring home to a friend or relative," Enrico said. "I'm the only one who sells high-end product. And I'm the only one with the money and connections to move the necklace as described by Captain Murino. But I never needed to work the black-market end of my business and pray I never will. I have yet to see that necklace, and the only time I see your goddaughter is when she passes my shop on her bike on her way to and from work."

"Which tells you what, old friend?" Nonna Maria asked.

"That if Loretta did steal the necklace, she still has it in her possession and doesn't know what to do with it," Enrico said. "That's one explanation."

"And a second?"

"That there never was a necklace for her or anyone else to steal," Enrico said.

13.

NONNA MARIA SAT on a straw chair, two rows from a closed curtain and a makeshift stage. Her seven-year-old granddaughter, Isabella, was nestled by her side, eager for the puppet show to begin. "If it gets scary, Nonna, don't worry," Isabella said. "I will keep you safe."

Nonna Maria rested a hand on the girl's knee and smiled. "I know you will," she said. "I can always count on you, Isabella."

The stage was situated between a bar/restaurant and the remnants of what had once been Jurassic Ischia, a failed attempt to turn the pine gardens, surrounded by acres of trees and pathways, into an amusement attraction. "You know, the puppets can't really talk, Nonna," Isabella said. "There is a man hiding behind the curtain who moves their mouths. He's the one who makes all the sounds."

"How do you know?" Nonna Maria asked, not bothering to hide her smile. "How do you know it's a man making them talk?"

"You can see his legs at the bottom of the curtains," Isabella said. "And you can see his hands pulling on the puppet strings."

Nonna Maria nodded. "Good thing you came with me, Isabella," she said. "If I came alone, I would not have known the truth of what happens behind the curtain."

Isabella sat quietly for a few moments, staring down at the dirt floor, ignoring the mingling of the small crowd sitting behind her, young and old alike, eager for the show to begin. "Can I ask you something, Nonna?" she asked.

"Anything," Nonna Maria said. "I keep no secrets from you."

"Is Loretta in trouble?" Isabella asked. "I heard Mama and Papa saying that the police think she took something from a woman at the hotel where she works. They are afraid she will go to jail. Is that true?"

"I know Loretta takes you to the beach when she's not working and spends time with you when your parents are away," Nonna Maria said. "Do you enjoy the time you spend with her?"

Isabella nodded. "Yes," she said. "She thinks up fun games for us to play and reads to me from story books she always carries in her bag. She even took me to see the puppet show here last summer. She's the one who told me about the man who makes the puppets move and talk."

"In the time you were with her, did Loretta ever take anything from you?" Nonna Maria asked. "A toy from your room or a book on your bed or money out of the back of the tiny elephant bank I gave you?"

"No, Nonna," Isabella said. "Never. She gives me things but she never took anything from me."

"I know, little one," Nonna Maria said. "And just like Loretta would never take anything from you, she would never take anything from anyone else. Especially a guest in the hotel where she works."

"So, why are they saying she did?"

"People say what they say for many reasons, little one," Nonna Maria said. "In time, we'll find out the truth. But for now, I don't want you to worry about Loretta. I'll keep her safe, just like you promised to keep me safe from the scary puppets we are about to see."

"Is the woman who says Loretta took something from her room a scary person?" Isabella asked.

Nonna Maria shook her head. "Not to me," she said. "I may be afraid of the puppets, but a woman like this signora doesn't bring me fear. She's a puzzle, and all that must be done is to put the pieces together. That's when we'll know the full story."

"Like the puzzles I put together in my room," Isabella said. "The ones Mama buys for me are hard and it takes a long time to put the pieces in place."

"The hardest puzzles take the longest time," Nonna Maria said. "But, in the end, it's time well spent."

14.

AN OAKEN COFFIN rested in the center of the old church, facing the altar and a somber-looking young priest. The rows of pews and straw-backed chairs were filled not with friends and family, but with curious strangers. A handful of elderly women, each dressed in widow's black, stood off to the sides, facing the silent statues of the saints staring down at them, lit candles dancing among the darkened shadows. In the rear of the church, standing a few steps removed from thick wooden doors, as much outside as in, Captain Murino and Nonna Maria watched in silence as the priest stepped down from the altar and blessed the coffin with holy water and recited a prayer of salvation for a woman he had never met.

"A funeral mass for a woman with no name, no identity," Captain Murino said. "Seems sad in so many unspeakable ways."

"The church could have let you wait a little longer," Nonna Maria said. "You might not have found out anything more than what you already know. But it would have been a kindness. Something you think a church would want to do for a woman who died on our island."

"It's a law, practically," Captain Murino said. "Not just on Ischia, but in all Italy. A body needs to be buried within twenty-four hours. As it was, the parish gave us an extra eight hours to try and sort things out."

"Where will she be buried?" Nonna Maria asked.

"At the local cemetery," Captain Murino said. "Temporarily. Until we get to the bottom of who she is, she'll rest in an unmarked grave."

Nonna Maria glanced over at Captain Murino and saw his youthful face filled with the weight of a sadness she had never seen in him before. "Do you know yet how she died?" she asked.

Captain Murino nodded. "We have a preliminary report," he said. "She was strangled and then tossed out on the street like a bag of garbage."

"So, she was not hit by a passing car?" Nonna Maria asked.

Captain Murino shook his head. "There is no indication that that occurred," he said. "She had a few bruises and some minor damage to her bones, but that most likely was caused by her being dropped to the ground. A car would have done much more serious damage."

Nonna Maria took a deep breath, turned from the doorway, and stepped into the full glare of a late morning sun. Captain Murino followed her into the warmth of the day. "I never imagined I would encounter a brutal crime such as the one before me here on Ischia," he said.

"There is evil everywhere, Captain," Nonna Maria said. "It is not, by any means, found only in big cities. The darkness is never far away."

"I've sent out requests to carabinieri offices in cities and towns from Naples to the Swiss border, asking for any information they might have on a missing woman fitting the victim's description," Captain Murino said. "No hits as of yet. And I have my men scouring not only Barano, but the other five boroughs as well. Not one clue has materialized that would lead us to this woman's identity."

"Someone knows, Captain," Nonna Maria said. "Someone always knows. This is an island of secrets and they are kept behind sealed lips. We each have them, everyone who lives here, and we choose never to speak of them."

"Even if it can help solve a murder?" Captain Murino asked.

"It depends on the secret and the one who is keeping it," Nonna Maria said. "I'm afraid some secrets remain buried forever. And not even the dead can bring them out into the open."

"I've been stationed here for six years, Nonna Maria," Captain Murino said. "But I don't think I'll ever fully understand this place and the people who live here."

"I've been here much longer, Captain," Nonna Maria said. "My bloodlines go back centuries. And still there are moments when I feel the same as you do. I've learned it is better to accept the people who make this island their home as they are rather than to judge them."

"Then I have the matter of the stolen necklace to deal with," Captain Murino said. "How is your goddaughter holding up?"

"She'll be better once the truth is known," Nonna Maria said.

Captain Murino allowed himself a slight smile. "And what truth would that be, Nonna Maria?" he asked.

"That she didn't steal the necklace," Nonna Maria said. "I don't know why this woman accused her. But that we will both come to know soon. You must never lose hope, Captain. It's one of the few things that give the poor and the innocent the strength to put one foot in front of the other and move forward. Without that feeling of hope, they would be lost."

"It would be nice to have some solid evidence to go along with those feelings of hope," Captain Murino said.

"That too will come your way, Captain," Nonna Maria said. "With time and a bit of patience. And, as with everything else we do together, we will both need a little help from some of our friends."

"You have me beat in that area, Nonna Maria," Captain Murino said. "I don't know anyone who has more friends than you do. There doesn't seem to be a single person on this island who doesn't know you, trust you, and count you as their friend."

"You're my friend too, Captain," Nonna Maria said. "And as you well know, I do everything I can to help my friends."

Captain Murino and Nonna Maria turned to look back toward the crowded church, the priest standing at the pulpit, talking in somber tones about loss and despair. Asking those in attendance to offer up a silent prayer for the soul of a woman whose name none of them knew. The people sitting side by side, in row after row, did not stir, heads up, hands folded, lips moving with silent words. The presence of a dead woman allowed, even briefly, to join in the hallowed company of too many loved ones no longer in their midst.

15.

THE TALL, MUSCULAR man sat across from Nonna Maria, watching as she poured him a second cup of espresso. "I made it strong," she said, placing the pot down in the center of a large tray filled with assorted cookies and pastries. "You might want to add an extra sugar."

"You always make strong coffee," the tall man, known throughout the island as Il Presidente, said. "Why should today be any different?"

"Have some cookies with your coffee," Nonna Maria said. "They're fresh out of the oven."

Il Presidente had been, in younger days, a man respected and feared. He was an intimidating figure who worked within a world of shadows, bringing with him a dark sense of danger. For years, his name was spoken in hushed tones, even among the criminal elements who ruled the streets of Naples, a city eighteen miles from Ischia's shores. He lived alone, shunned by members of his own family, lost in the bleakness of a profession that often ended in bloodshed and brutality.

But as the years passed, the men who ruled those streets were either found dead in the middle of one or sent away to prison for decades. As Il Presidente himself grew older, a new generation of criminals replaced those who departed, and they brought in a new crop of men willing to do the work he had once so effortlessly done and, more often than not, at a lesser price than he charged. There was no shortage of savagery in their profession, and Il Presidente was, in short order, a figure remembered and feared only in legend.

In his later years, he found himself lost and abandoned, a recluse living on an island paradise whose citizens steered clear of the man whose very name had once caused them to tremble. He drifted from one dank dwelling to another, still living within the shadows, but now with little in the way of employment or money, waiting out his remaining days a haunted man.

Nonna Maria never feared Il Presidente.

She was aware of the muscle work he had once done, a living earned in a profession tinged with blood, in a world populated by violent men. But she also knew there was more to the man than the fear he inspired in his youth and the pity he encountered in his later years. He was a solitary man, even in his prime, and had long ago buried the sadness of his early life, keeping the pain and anguish he had endured locked beneath his silent veneer. His childhood was a secret to all, but not to Nonna Maria.

She knew all about the horror endured by Il Presidente's mother, a childhood friend of Nonna Maria. She had been a petite young woman, shy and devoted to her family and her religion. She had plans to become a nun and traveled by boat to Pompeii to meet with the Mother Superior at the all-girls orphanage there. She missed her connecting train from Naples to Pompeii, traveling alone, her first time off the island. The next train was not scheduled to leave for another hour, and the young woman decided to use the time to explore Naples, a city she had heard only dire warnings about from her parents.

Those warnings proved, in her case, tragically true. The young woman, confused by the traffic and the crowds, ventured into an area she should have avoided. She was lost, the afternoon sun disappearing into the edges of the bay replaced by darkness, the train to Pompeii long departed.

The young woman disappeared, vanished as if she never existed. Her frantic parents, upon receiving word from the orphanage that their daughter had never arrived for her visit, traveled to Naples and got in touch with the local authorities. Despite their best efforts, the young woman was never found. It would be ten years before she returned to the island of Ischia, with a young son clutching onto the side of her dress. She had long ago abandoned any thoughts of entering a church, let alone a convent, and had aged considerably in her decade away from home.

She related her tale of misery and woe to the members of her family, not shying away from the sad details of the life she had been forced into for the past years, the humiliations she endured, the faceless men she encountered, the abuse she absorbed. And then, her final and frantic escape from the clutches of evil hands and back to the only place she had ever considered her home.

The young woman had expected to be embraced and forgiven. Instead she was shunned, both she and her son cast out, a disgrace to the family name. She moved to an isolated part of Ischia Ponte and earned a meager living by selling handmade trinkets by day, making enough to keep herself and her son in food and clothing. The boy attended school for a brief period, but the steady barrage of ridicule and fighting forced him to leave. On the eve of his sixteenth birthday, the young man who would soon develop both a fearsome reputation and a name he would carry for the rest of his life—Il Presidente—made his decision: If he was going to be shut out of ordinary civilian life, he would make his place in its darkest corners. Then those who had mocked him would one day grow to fear him.

Nonna Maria, back then a married woman with a growing family, did all she could to help the woman and her son. She brought food and clothing that her sons had outgrown and left them in front of the dank basement door that opened into the one-room apartment the two called home. She pleaded with the woman's family to forgive their daughter and embrace their grandson, but to no avail.

The young woman succumbed to illness and died before her thirty-fifth birthday, a life of promise lived out under a blanket of darkness. Il Presidente left Ischia and built his frightful reputation, returning decades later to live as his mother had lived, hidden by shadows and away from prying eyes. But he never forgot the kindness Nonna Maria had shown both to his mother and himself, and when she turned to him for help, he never hesitated.

He now lived on the first floor of Nonna Maria's home, tending to her garden and helping with household chores and, when the need arose, protecting her from anyone who sought to bring her harm. He had finally found peace, on an island he once despised, in the company of an old woman he had always respected and had now grown to love.

His meals were either brought down to him or he went up to the second floor to sit at Nonna Maria's table and devour whatever feast she had prepared. On those occasions, she would sit across from him, sipping either her coffee or a glass of wine, each finding comfort in the other's company.

Il Presidente had, at long last, found a home.

16.

NONNA MARIA WATCHED as Il Presidente downed his second cup of coffee, and she pushed the plate filled with cookies and pastries closer to him. "Take as many as you want with you," she said. "In case you get hungry later."

"I have been living in your home for close to a year," Il Presidente said to her, "and not once have I seen you eat anything, not even a piece of bread. Is it because you prefer to eat alone?"

"I never eat alone," Nonna Maria said. She was sitting in her usual place, on a wooden chair facing a large wood-framed photo of her late husband, Gabriel, that hung in the middle of a whitewashed wall directly behind Il Presidente. "I sit here and eat in the company of my husband. We always had our meals together, the two of us, even when the children were small. We would feed them first, get them cleaned up and ready for bed. And then we would sit down, me here and him seated where you are. It was our time together. And it still is. Alive or dead, it still is."

"He was a good man, your husband," Il Presidente said. "He was kind to me and to my mother. And to many others, both on this island and beyond."

Nonna Maria stared up at her husband's framed photo and nodded. "You heard about the woman's body found in Barano?" she asked.

"Yes," Il Presidente said. "Known to no one, at least that's what is being said. No identification, a body without a name or a history."

"Everyone has a name and a history," Nonna Maria said. "Some, for reasons of their own, decide to hide it."

"I could get in touch with some friends in Naples," Il Presidente said. "See if they know anything about her. Give them a description and see where it leads."

Nonna Maria shook her head. "I don't think the answers we need will be found in Naples," she said. "This woman came to Ischia for a reason, and once we know what that reason is, then all the pieces will fall in place."

"What do you need me to do?" Il Presidente asked.

"Her body was found on a street in Barano," Nonna Maria said. "So, whatever she came to find must be there. She may have family on this island, but for whatever motive, they may want to keep that fact a secret."

Il Presidente smiled. "I know that feeling all too well," he said.

"Sadly, you do," Nonna Maria said. "We need to find that family and discover the reason they haven't come forward."

"That could mean the secret is deeply personal," Il Presidente said. "It must be more than a simple feud or a disagreement over property or money."

"There's always someone who knows the reason behind the silence," Nonna Maria said. "And that's who we need to find."

17.

CAPTAIN MURINO AND Nonna Maria stood on the Lido, looking out at the waters of the bay. It was a cloudless early summer morning, the heat not yet at its zenith, a steady stream of waves splashing against the black rocks jutting out to sea. "The sea always looks peaceful from here," the captain said. "It's one of my favorite places on the island."

"My husband loved it too," Nonna Maria said. "We would often take long walks here at night, talking about our days or just walking without saying a word. I will always remember those walks."

"I know you miss your husband very much," the captain said. "He was lucky to have you in his life."

"We were both lucky, Captain," Nonna Maria said. "We had many wonderful years together, and as long as the memories are with me, so is my Gabriel."

"Signora Conte stopped by the station house earlier and filed a formal complaint," the captain said. "She named Loretta as the one who stole her necklace."

"Anything else?" Nonna Maria asked.

"She also requested that the hotel reimburse her for her stay and other expenses she incurred," Captain Murino said. "And she asked for a copy of the complaint to be sent on to her insurance company."

"Do you believe her?" Nonna Maria asked. "That she had a valuable necklace stolen from her room?"

"I have concerns," Captain Murino said. "No one at the hotel, none of the other guests, none of the taxi drivers who drove Signora Conte to various spots on the island, not a single one recalls seeing her wearing a necklace of any kind. And I made a point of bringing that to her attention."

"And what did she say?" Nonna Maria asked.

"She told me she always travels with it," the captain said. "It is her most prized possession. She does not think of it as a piece of jewelry to be worn and shown. It is her inheritance and a reminder of the loved ones who left it to her."

"I feel the same way about my espresso pot," Nonna Maria said. "It is the first gift my husband gave me. It is the reason I drink only coffee poured from that pot. But I don't carry it with me everywhere I go."

"Signora Conte has extended her stay at the hotel," Captain Murino said, "until this matter is settled. And, given the circumstances, the hotel manager is not charging her for the additional time."

"Did she tell you what the necklace looked like?" Nonna Maria asked.

"In detail," Captain Murino said. "Eighteen pearl ringlets held together by a gold chain. It was a gift to her grandmother from a commissioned officer assigned to the Vatican consulate in Rome. My men are checking whether there are existing records of a necklace such as the one she described as well as locating the name of the officer. But I doubt they will find anything. Many years have passed."

"Did she show you photos of the necklace?" Nonna Maria asked.

"She had only one," the captain said. "A photo of her mother, in an evening gown, wearing the necklace. Her mother was barely out of her twenties when the photo was taken, so, again, the timeline presents an issue."

"What does Signora Conte want?" Nonna Maria asked.

Captain Murino stopped and turned to face Nonna Maria. "I assume she wants her necklace returned to her," he said.

"And if it's not?"

"She says it's insured for three hundred thousand euros," the captain said. "We're looking into that. If that proves to be the case, the insurance company will have to pay her. If it is insured, then that tells me she is not lying about owning a necklace such as the one described. An insurance company would not allow her to take out a policy without proof of its existence."

Nonna Maria shrugged. "I know nothing about insurance," she said. "But I know my cousin Aldo, dead now for many years, had his car insured, and every so often he would put in whatever it is you put in when you want money from an insurance company."

"A claim," Captain Murino said.

"He would put that in, send some photos to the company showing the damage, and attach a bill," Nonna Maria said. "A few weeks later, a check came to him in the mail, covering most of the amount."

"That's how it's supposed to work, Nonna Maria," Captain Murino said. "Other than the insurance company sending an investigator to inspect the damage, especially if the claim was for a significant amount."

"All the requests Aldo put in were for small amounts," Nonna Maria said. "He wasn't looking to draw attention. The insurance company was based outside of Naples, and it was cheaper for them to pay than to send someone to Ischia to look into what the photos and the bill revealed to be a minor accident."

"And your point in telling me this is what?" Captain Murino asked.

"My cousin Aldo never owned a car," Nonna Maria said. "He never even knew how to drive. The bills he wrote were on forms he got from a friend's garage. Aldo always carried a small camera with him, and whenever he saw a car in a particular color and style like the one he claimed he owned with some minor damage, he would stop and take photos. He then put in his claim, as you call it, and collected the money."

"But he would have to pay for the insurance," Captain Murino said. "It would be difficult for him to turn a profit."

"Not if he had a friend working at the insurance company who took care of the paperwork," Nonna Maria said.

"So, you think Signora Conte filed false insurance documents?" Captain Murino asked. "That she's lying about the necklace and the insurance policy?"

"No," Nonna Maria said. "I was telling you about my cousin Aldo to show you there are many ways to skin a rabbit."

"A cat," Captain Murino said. "Not a rabbit."

"In the North, it might be cats," Nonna Maria said. "But in the South, we prefer rabbits."

Captain Murino nodded. "Signora Conte would also like some sort of settlement from the hotel."

"What kind of settlement?" Nonna Maria asked.

"The only kind that matters, Nonna Maria," the captain said. "A financial one."

"And she will remain in Ischia, as a guest of the hotel," Nonna Maria said.

"That's her plan," Captain Murino said.

"There are two people who know the truth, Captain," Nonna Maria said. "My goddaughter. And Signora Conte. And one of them is lying."

Captain Murino smiled. "And I have little doubt, Nonna Maria, which of the two you think is the liar."

Nonna Maria nodded. "Maybe," she said. "But I need the same thing you need, and that's proof."

"It's going to be a very hot day, Nonna Maria," Captain Murino said, watching as she picked up her black tote bag and turned to walk back home. "Try to stay out of the sun if you can."

"My nephew the doctor tells me the same thing," Nonna Maria said. "But he also tells me the warm sun is good for my muscle aches. It's not easy to do both. Especially at my age."

"You have an answer for everything, Nonna Maria," Captain Murino said.

"Not everything, Captain," Nonna Maria said. "I still don't know whether a necklace was stolen. And I still don't know who killed an unknown woman in Barano."

Captain Murino looked surprised by her response. "I didn't know the case in Barano was of interest to you, Nonna Maria," he said. "I thought you only got involved in matters to help your friends."

"Here in Ischia, Captain Murino, everyone is my friend," Nonna Maria said.

She turned and walked slowly down the Lido, tote bag now flung over her right shoulder, the sun at her back.

18.

THE STREGA SAT in a dimly lit room, her back to an open window, humid air filtering through two thin white curtains. She was a robust woman with gnarled hands and a face that had spent many years shielded from daylight. Her eyes were the color of Greek olives and her gray hair was thick and in need of a wash and a comb. She wore a rumpled blue dress and rested her bare feet on the worn wooden slabs of a thick table covered by a red-and-white checkered cloth. There were two large lit candles resting in the center of the table and between them a large white porcelain bowl containing water, olive oil, and the eyes of a goat. She rested her hands flat on the table and looked over at Nonna Maria. "It has been a long time since you have come to see me," she said. "But you have never been one to seek answers from someone like me."

"I'm not," Nonna Maria said. "But I know that many on Ischia do. That is why I have come."

"If you are expecting me to tell you about anyone who has been in the chair you are now sitting in, you have lived long enough to know that is not something I can do," the Strega said.

"The words spoken in this room never leave it. I take my premonitions to my grave."

"You have heard about the woman found on the road?" Nonna Maria asked.

The Strega nodded. "It is a sad tale," she said. "Such a death is a rare occurrence in Ischia."

"Did you know this woman?" Nonna Maria asked. "Has she ever set foot inside this room?"

"I told you I cannot reveal what words were spoken in the privacy of this chamber," the Strega said.

"I didn't ask you to tell me what she said," Nonna Maria said. "I asked if you knew her and if she had ever been to see you. If not recently, then maybe some years back."

"Why do you need to know?" the Strega asked. "This woman means nothing to you. She's not family. I know you are one to get involved in other people's lives. But never for a stranger, and that is what this woman is to you. Nothing more."

"This poor woman is now resting in an unmarked grave," Nonna Maria said. "She may have been put there by someone who makes his home on our island. If that is the case, then she was put there for a reason. Perhaps for a secret that the one who killed her cannot risk being known. "

"And you came here thinking I know something about this unfortunate incident?" the Strega said.

"Many people on the island come to see you," Nonna Maria said. "They pay good money to have you look in that bowl, close your eyes and pretend you see what will happen to them, both good and bad. And they believe what you tell them."

"But you do not," the Strega said.

"Many find comfort in the words you pass on to them and if it helps, that's a good thing," Nonna Maria said. "Whether I believe it or not doesn't matter."

The Strega stayed silent for a few moments, her eyes focused on Nonna Maria. She drew in a deep and congested breath before she spoke. "If I help you in any way, it cannot ever pass your lips that I spoke to you," she said. "People trust me to keep their secrets. It would ruin me."

"You know everything there is to know about me," Nonna Maria said. "And one of the things you know is I can be trusted."

"I know you are friendly with the carabinieri captain," the Strega said. "And that you often work together. He's a stranger to me and I cannot risk having my words reach his ears."

"I will only tell him what I know," Nonna Maria said. "Not who it was that told me."

"I don't know the dead woman," the Strega said. "I've never met her, nor has she ever been to see me."

Nonna Maria leaned in closer to the table, rested both her hands on the Strega's, and asked, "What do you know?"

"There has been talk that the woman returned to Ischia for a reason," the Strega said, speaking in hushed tones. "Returned to see what she had been forced to leave behind many years ago."

"What was it?" Nonna Maria asked.

"Keep in mind, this is only talk," the Strega said. "There may not be an ounce of truth to any of it."

"Tell me, anyway," Nonna Maria said.

"This woman had a secret," the Strega said. "According to

what I've heard, she had kept it for over twenty years. It was that secret that led her back home, back to Ischia. And that secret may have led to her death."

"Do you know what the secret is?" Nonna Maria asked.

"It's possible the woman came back to see a child," the Strega said. "A child she had been forced to abandon. She might have returned to see her now as a grown woman with a daughter of her own. That is as much as I've heard and as much as I can pass on."

19.

ARIANNA CONTE WAS walking slowly over a small wooden bridge in La Mortella Gardens, her right arm resting under the bent elbow of a tall, distinguished-looking man in his late fifties. He had a thick mane of white hair, kept long at the back and sides, and was wearing a long-sleeved white cotton shirt, white cargo shorts, and brown loafers. His name was Guido Bernardino, and he was Arianna Conte's occasional business partner in a variety of ventures, a few of them legal, many of them on the shady side.

"It was both a surprise and a pleasure to hear from you," he said to her, his voice soaked in the dialect of his native city of Milan. "I didn't think you ventured this far south to pursue your little adventures."

"It was an impulse decision, I admit," Arianna said. "I thought the island would be both relaxing and rewarding. It has, to this moment, proved to be neither."

"Your chosen target was a good one," Bernardino said. "A five-star hotel catering to wealthy tourists. No security cameras of any worth anywhere on the grounds. A dedicated staff and a manager who will go to great lengths to avoid causing any embarrassment to the hotel. What am I missing?"

"For one thing, I misjudged the local carabinieri," Arianna said. "I had heard they send raw recruits to the island to get them used to the work, knowing they would not be assigned anything close to a major crime or theft. That may be true of the lower-ranking officers, but not of the captain. While he has been stationed here for six years, he is from the North and is neither a fool nor inexperienced."

"And your target?" Bernardino asked. "Has she been detained?"

"She has been questioned and is under house arrest," Arianna said. "She poses no flight risk and has no criminal record. Normally, that would work in my favor. The hotel would look to make a quick settlement and I would be well on my way off the island."

"But . . ."

"There's a meddlesome old woman involved," Arianna said. "She has the ear of the captain. And she has involved herself in the investigation. Not in any way you would notice, but she seems to have connections throughout the island and they all seem eager to offer their help. I hear she has a personal stake in the matter. The young cleaning lady is her goddaughter."

"There is still a necklace missing," Bernardino said. "And someone accused of taking it. Both the old woman and the carabinieri captain need to prove a theft did not happen. Perhaps it has taken longer than you would like for it to come to its fitting conclusion. But we have been involved in enough of these escapades to know that sooner rather than later the hotel will have no choice but to buy your silence. The only question that remains is how high the offer."

It was warm in this section of the gardens, a tropical paradise featuring flowers from around the world, and they ventured around several bends to an area offering a cooler climate. La Mortella Gardens was once privately owned but had since been left to the island for the public to walk through and enjoy. It is favored more by the tourists than the locals and is a jumping-off point for many to venture from its well-maintained grounds over to Poseidon to spend the rest of their day enjoying the thermal spa and bath treatments that that resort offered.

"You are probably correct and it will all come to a profitable conclusion," Arianna said. "But I need to cover myself in the event it doesn't end as I had originally planned."

"What do you need me to do?" Bernardino asked.

"I need you to get me a necklace, very much like the one I described to the carabinieri and hotel staff," Arianna said. "And I need it to be placed where the finger of guilt clearly points to the cleaning woman. This way, no matter how suspicious the carabinieri captain is and how much information this old woman can dig up, there can be no doubt a crime was committed and the cleaning woman is a thief. Just as I initially reported."

"I'm not looking to put a young woman behind bars, Arianna," Bernardino said. "Nor, in any way, am I your accomplice in this matter. I can get you a necklace, similar in style to the one reported stolen. That can be done in a day, two at the most. I am more than happy to help you in that regard. But as to helping to frame the cleaning girl, that is above my pay grade, so to speak. It is not what I do. I'm afraid you must either handle that end on your own or get in touch with someone else who can be of help."

Arianna looked away from a large tropical plant and over at Bernardino. "You will help me on both matters," she said, her tone harsher, her words spoken with a hint of defiance. "You have no choice."

Bernardino narrowed his gaze on Arianna and stared at her for a moment. "The next hydrofoil leaves for Naples in less than an hour," he said. "I plan to be on it. As to your necklace, once I have it in my possession, I'll get word to you through a third party and you will let him know the best means of getting the piece to you. That is my choice."

"If you don't agree to help me in both areas and my situation worsens, I may need to cut a deal," Arianna said, still holding her gaze. "If that's the case, you're my bargaining chip, Guido, and a good one to have, I might add. I would prefer not to have to give you up, seeing as how we have been doing business together for so many years. But ours is not a business built on friendship, only on need. So, will you help me or not?"

Bernardino looked to his left and to his right before responding. "I'll help you," he said. "Reluctantly I'll do as you ask. But remember, I know as much about you as you do about me. You've been pulling your cons for a long time and I've been there for most of them, and what I haven't witnessed I've heard about. So, I can make a deal with the carabinieri captain just as easily as you can. And, given the circumstances, there's a better than even chance he will prefer my tale to yours."

"In that case, we both run a risk," Arianna said. "When you return to Ischia with the necklace, steer clear of the port area and book yourself in an out-of-the-way hotel."

"I know how the game is played," Bernardino said. "We

meet as we first met this morning, at the coffee shop across from the port, you at one table, me at another."

They resumed their walk, her arm once again entwined with his. Arianna glanced at her watch and then looked at Bernardino. "I would ask you to stay for lunch," she said, "but there's not much time. You have a hydrofoil to catch and a necklace to either steal or purchase."

"Fair enough," Bernardino said. "Just one final thing I should mention before I head off."

"Make it quick," Arianna said.

"After this escapade of yours is complete," Bernardino said, "you and I are finished. I assume you will continue doing what you do. You're very good at it, despite this slight hiccup. But, find yourself another partner."

"Because I threatened you?" Arianna said. "I never took you for the sensitive type."

"I've worked with you, Arianna, because you have, for many years, made it profitable for me," Bernardino said. "But I never liked you. And after today, I am well aware I can't trust you. Combine those two factors and it makes me realize the risk is not worth the reward."

Bernardino smiled and nodded at Arianna, then turned and began his walk out of La Mortella Gardens to where a taxi waited to take him back to the port.

20.

NONNA MARIA SAT at a corner table at Da Salvatore's restaurant, staring out at the rush of waves beating against the clear sand. It was a warm, humid morning, and overhead a cluster of thick dark clouds brought with them the threat of an afternoon storm. She sat alone; the owners, Salvatore and his son, Giorgio, were busy tying down the beach umbrellas and folding up the lounge chairs, in anticipation of the bad weather to come.

She looked out at the rough waters, her mind racing back decades, recalling a memory she had long ago buried in her past. A memory of a friend she had not been able to help, despite her attempts. A friend who was banished from Ischia for the simple crime of falling in love with the wrong man.

Ischia, as modern as it might seem to the outside observer, filled with high-end boutiques, Michelin-starred restaurants, and hotels that cater to the celebrated and the wealthy, is to this day an island locked in its ways. For many of the locals, the customs and habits of old maintain a strong grip. Men live at home and do not leave until they are married, and even then, they don't venture far, usually living in a nearby apartment left to them by a relative. If they lack such good fortune, they continue to live with their elders, waiting out the years until the home is theirs alone.

They are taught from a young age to marry a girl who will not bring shame to the family name, the clear implication being that the bride is expected to be a virgin on her wedding night. Anything less would be scandalous. And while many of the men keep mistresses, his wife is expected to bear his children and be faithful only to the man whose ring she wears.

A mistress can be kept for many years, loved from a distance, ridiculed by those in the know, but must never attempt to break apart a marriage. And she is expected never to bear her lover a child. It would bring her only misery and ruin.

Nonna Maria was friendly with one such woman, and as she watched the waves splash their mist closer to her table, she thought back to the events that led to her being cast aside, as if her life had no meaning. And the child she bore never knew her true mother.

The woman's name was Fernanda Matturana.

She was younger than Nonna Maria, back then a young girl who fell under the spell of a married man and believed his lies that he would leave his wife, abandon his family to start a life with her. Nonna Maria, then a wife and a mother to a family of seven, did her best to persuade the young girl to break off with the married man and free herself from his grip.

"He will never leave his wife and children, Fernanda," Nonna Maria had said to her as they walked together down the sloping Via Roma, passing clothing stores, gelato stands, a barbershop, and table-lined trattorias. "Not for you or for any other woman."

"He says he loves me," Fernanda said, her voice filled with youthful passion. "He says he loves only me."

"You are not the first one to hear him speak those words," Nonna Maria said. "He has had many women in the years since he took his wedding vows. They all believed him. Yet he still lives at home with his family."

"It will be different with me," Fernanda said. "None of those women gave him what I am going to give him."

"What's that?"

"A child, Maria," Fernanda said. "I am pregnant with his child."

Nonna Maria stopped and turned to face the young woman. "Does he know?" she asked. "Does he know you are carrying his child?"

Fernanda shook her head and smiled. "Not yet," she said. "I'm meeting him later tonight, on the walkway to the Castello. I wanted to make sure before I told him. I saw the doctor earlier this morning and he confirmed what I already knew to be true."

"You can't let him know," Nonna Maria said. "He is not the type of man to do right by you. You will be running a great risk by telling him."

"But he is the father of my child," Fernanda said. "He has a right to know."

"With most men that would be true," Nonna Maria said. "But Carlo is not like most men. Open your eyes, Fernanda, and think long and hard about what you are about to do."

"You don't know him the way I do," Fernanda said.

"I know him better than you think I do," Nonna Maria said. "Carlo comes off as a caring and loving man. But that's a mask.

Take that away and what's behind it is a dangerous man who will do anything not to lose the comfortable life he has. A life that's come to him not through hard work, but from the pockets of his mother and father. They are the ones who feed and clothe his children. They are the ones who buy his groceries and pay for his cigarettes and gambling debts. They are the ones who keep his wife company while he spends his nights with other women, pretending they are unaware of their son's habits."

"But what about the baby?" Fernanda asked. "Soon people will know I am with child. It can only be hidden for so long. I will be a single woman with a baby and no husband I can point to and no father I can name. You know what will be said about me and my baby. First in whispers and then in voices loud enough to be heard."

"I will help you," Nonna Maria said. "I will find a way for you to have the baby and leave Carlo's name out of it."

Fernanda shook her head and started to walk away from Nonna Maria. "There is only one way, Maria," she said. "And that is for Carlo to keep his promise to me. Accept me as the woman he loves and the baby I carry as his child."

Nonna Maria had stood in the middle of Via Roma and watched Fernanda Matturana walk down the street toward the port.

It was the last time she would ever see her.

But she had heard the rumors that spread like a winter fire. Fernanda had her child in Naples, but she never returned to Ischia. Around the time that she would have given birth, Carlo's wife came home from Naples with a newborn in her arms. This despite the fact no one, not even members of her own family, were aware she had been pregnant. The baby, a girl, was named Assunta, and she is now herself a young woman, working in Forio for a local bank.

Summer rainstorms in Ischia always arrive with a sudden fury, and as the heavy drops hit the wide umbrella covering Nonna Maria's table with a force that threatened to lift it off its moorings, she seemed not to notice.

Salvatore waved at her from outside the glass enclosure of his restaurant. "Come in and stay with us," he shouted. "Otherwise we may lose you to the sea."

Nonna Maria shook her head. "I've always liked the rain," she said to him. "It helps cool the air and send the heat and humidity toward Capri."

Salvatore smiled and stepped back into his restaurant. "If you need anything, you know where to find me," he said.

Nonna Maria sat back in her white plastic chair, puddles forming around her feet, rainwater filtering down from the sides of the umbrella onto her arms and shoulders. Her mind stayed focused on a friend she had not seen for decades. A friend Nonna Maria had always felt she had not done enough to help when she was at her most vulnerable. Was it possible that Fernanda had returned to Ischia after all these years? To finally see a daughter she had left behind to be raised by another woman? Raised by a man she loved and who, she once believed, loved her in turn?

Could the body of the woman found on that road in Barano, murdered and abandoned like a pile of garbage, be that of Fernanda Matturana? There was no way yet for Nonna Maria to know for certain. There were many other young women in those years who found themselves in similar circumstances as her friend, forced to leave Ischia out of a combination of fear and shame.

Nonna Maria sat under that umbrella for several hours, long after the storm clouds passed and the sun once again began to shine. And all during that time, she sat in silence, staring out at the rough waters of a roiled bay, the tears streaming down her face mixing with the raindrops coursing along her wrinkled skin.

The tears she shed were fueled not just by sadness and remorse, but also by anger at the unfairness of a life so recklessly ruined.

If it was the body of Fernanda Matturana that had been found on the side of the road, then Nonna Maria would set out to do for her in death what she could not do for her friend in life.

She would help find her killer and tell her daughter the truth about her real mother.

Fernanda would, at long last, get the justice she deserved.

21.

ARIANNA CONTE SAT at an outside table on the terrace of the Excelsior Hotel. The heavy downpour earlier in the day had brought forth a warm and sunny afternoon. Signora Conte was grateful for the shade the terrace offered. She glanced down at the thermal pool off to her right, a dozen sunbathers lounging on the chairs ringing the pool while three teenagers stood chest-deep in the water, talking quietly, occasionally splashing water onto their shoulders and necks. A thin waiter stepped in front of her and poured a glass of mineral water and quietly opened a bottle of Casa D'Ambra vino bianco. "In this weather, a nice, cool glass of wine is just what is needed," the waiter said, his voice soft, his manner that of a man who had served hundreds in his years working at the hotel.

"A cool glass of wine is always needed," Arianna Conte said. "No matter the weather."

"Agreed," the waiter said with a smile. "And have you decided what you would like for lunch?"

"I'll check out your buffet," Arianna said. "But not right now. I'd like to sit and enjoy my wine and water for a bit."

"As you wish," the waiter said and moved away in the silence of his practiced profession.

"It's not a good idea to drink on an empty stomach," Nonna Maria said. She was standing slightly behind Arianna, the cool of the interior dining room at her back, facing the pool below. "That's what I've always been told, though I do it myself."

Arianna stared up at Nonna Maria for a moment and then gestured with her right hand for her to sit. "Join me," she said. "And have some wine and some lunch to go with it. My treat, of course."

"I drink my wine when the sun goes down," Nonna Maria said. She pulled back an iron chair with a soft cushion and sat across from Arianna.

"A glass of water, then," Arianna said.

"It would be a waste of the water," Nonna Maria said. "I have a number of bad habits, but drinking water has never been one of them."

Arianna smiled and sat back, her wineglass cupped in both hands. "I was hoping you and I would meet," she said. "Perhaps the two of us can settle this matter of my necklace and save the carabinieri from wasting any more of their time."

"The carabinieri will continue to do what they do," Nonna Maria said. "And I will continue to do what I do."

"And what is it, exactly," Arianna asked, "that you do?"

"In this case, I'm going to clear the name of a young woman who I believe you have falsely accused of stealing a necklace," Nonna Maria said.

"She is related to you in some way," Arianna said. "Or so I've been led to believe."

"Loretta is my goddaughter," Nonna Maria said. "And she is not a thief."

"I would expect you to say that," Arianna said. "But the necklace is missing and she has been snooping around my room. She admits so herself. Has told both the carabinieri and the hotel manager that she has been in my room a number of times each day."

"She would have been fired for not doing her duties if she weren't in your room every day," Nonna Maria said. "It is her job to help clean your room and to check if the minibar has been used and to then prepare the room for the evening."

Arianna took a long sip of her wine and nodded. "I see you have been made aware of her work routine," she said. "And, of course, I'm sure you've spent time in a number of hotels yourself."

"I've never stayed at a hotel," Nonna Maria said. "But I did put in a good word for Loretta with the hotel manager when she first applied for her job. He's an old family friend and knew she would work hard and could be trusted. And that held true until you came along."

"She sounds like a sensible young woman," Arianna said. "But even someone like her can fall prey to temptation. We all, at one time or another, do things we later come to regret."

Nonna Maria looked at Arianna, her eyes catching the bracelets wrapped around both her wrists and the emerald earrings hanging off each lobe. Her blond hair was combed straight back and held in place by two thick silver clips. She was wearing a blue sundress and had her legs crossed under the table.

"Loretta did not steal your necklace, Signora Conte," Nonna Maria said after a few moments. "It would not be possible for her to take something that I believe doesn't exist."

"So, your goddaughter is not a thief, but I am a liar," Arianna said. "May I ask how you arrived at such a conclusion?"

"One of my granddaughters loves magic tricks," Nonna Maria said. "Always has. And she's become very good at doing them herself. She studies different magicians from all over the world, all on this little machine she carries around with her. Then she learns how to do the tricks herself and does them for me."

"Your granddaughter sounds as if she's on her way to a career in magic," Arianna said. "Good for her. But that has nothing to do with me, my necklace, or what you sit here and accuse me of."

"She doesn't want to be a magician," Nonna Maria said. "Stella wants to be a surgeon. But she enjoys watching the magic tricks. And she has learned an important lesson from them."

"And what would that be?"

"She told me it's not a trick that the magician performs," Nonna Maria said. "She said it is an illusion. He wants you to believe you just saw a trick. A rabbit pulled from a hat or a person cut in half. But none of that ever happened. The trick is to make us believe it did. And that's what you're doing with Loretta. A magic trick. Making a necklace disappear. A necklace that never existed."

"You are a clever old woman," Arianna said. "And I have no doubt you can spin a few tricks of your own. But your tricks won't work on me."

Nonna Maria pushed back her chair and stood. "I'm taking you away from your lunch," she said. "The chef here is excellent and her buffet is one of the best on the island."

"A wonderful review from someone who has never stayed at a hotel," Arianna said with a smile.

"People like to talk," Nonna Maria said. "And, at times, I listen. It's a habit and one I'm too old to break."

"I'm glad you came and found me," Arianna said. "I've heard quite a bit about you from both the hotel manager and the carabinieri captain. They both speak highly of you."

"It helps to be old," Nonna Maria said. "It's hard for anyone to not speak highly of the old. They never know how much longer we'll be around."

22.

PEPE THE PAINTER was at his usual post on Corso Vittoria Colonna, an array of his portraits and landscapes lined up against the base of the white stucco walls of the Villa Angela. He was an Ischia fixture and sold his works to both tourists looking to take a memory of Ischia back home with them and the locals for whom he painted portraits of their children and parents. He was a tall, robust man with a thick mane of white hair and a beard that matched. He began his workday around sundown and continued well into the early morning hours, especially during the spring and summer seasons when the streets could always be counted on to be filled with tourists.

He wore white pants with the cuffs rolled and a white shirt with the sleeves turned up to his elbows. He would drive to the Corso from his small home in the hills of Barano. It was a home filled with his work—paints in dozens of colors; small and large canvases; color photos of landscapes; old, thick books filled with the history of Ischia told in pictures.

The home was also filled with memories—it was where Pepe the Painter had lived with his late wife, Elena, for more than three decades, sharing the many happy times those years brought them, followed by a few years of sadness when he watched helplessly as his wife surrendered to a disease that no amount of medicine or prayer could cure.

Pepe the Painter spent as little time in the house as possible. The passing years had not eased the pain of his loss, and he found his only solace in his work and in the company of the friends he had scattered throughout the island.

And among those friends was the one he liked and trusted the most—Nonna Maria.

Pepe the Painter smiled and clapped his hands happily when he saw Nonna Maria approach. They had been friends since both were in the prime of life, first brought together by Nonna Maria's marriage to his cousin, Gabriel, a good and gentle man brought down by the same disease that stole his wife from his side.

"If I was a man who prayed, I would pray that you brought something delicious for me to eat and something cold for me to drink," Pepe the Painter said to Nonna Maria as she stepped up to his work station.

"I brought enough for two meals," Nonna Maria said. "You can choose between an eggplant parmigiana panino and marinated artichokes, or pasta with oil, garlic, and broccoli rabe for your dinner tonight. The other you can save for your lunch tomorrow. I also have some of those stuffed zucchini flowers you like, as well as some prosciutto and a slab of cheese."

"If my stomach had arms it would hug you," Pepe the Painter said, taking the heavy tote bag from Nonna Maria.

"There's a bottle of D'Ambra red and a chilled white in there as well," Nonna Maria said. "There's some coffee, and two bottles of mineral water that my nephew the doctor insists on having delivered to my home each week."

"He cares for you, your nephew," Pepe the Painter said. "He wants you to stay hydrated."

"Whatever that means, I'm pretty sure I can get it from drinking coffee and wine," Nonna Maria said.

"Sit with me, Nonna Maria, while I choose from the feast you prepared," Pepe said, pulling a wooden folding chair from behind a counter crammed with paints and brushes. He opened the chair and placed it next to his, resting the black tote bag between them.

Nonna Maria sat and glanced out at the passing throng of tourists mingled with locals. She pulled out a folded handkerchief and wiped the sweat forming on her upper lip. "This season is even more crowded than last year," she said. "It seems each year that passes, more and more people come to the island. For so many years, very few came. Now there aren't enough boats to bring them all here."

"There are moments when I prefer it the way it used to be," Pepe the Painter said. "Back then we made a lot less money, but we had our island to ourselves. I'm not quite sure the trade-off has been worth it."

"The younger ones don't remember those years as we do," Nonna Maria said. "They have grown up knowing Ischia only as an island filled with rich tourists in the summer and a few quiet months in the winter. And for them, it's all for the better."

"Better or not, it's their turn at the wheel now," Pepe the Painter said, reaching into the tote bag and pulling out a large panino. "Our future is behind us."

Nonna Maria looked at the landscapes and portraits lining the walls of the Villa Angela. "You have been painting since we first met," she said. "You also took photos in those years, if my memory hasn't left me for a sharper mind."

"No one's mind is sharper than yours, Nonna Maria," Pepe the Painter said as he took a large bite of the panino. "I worked as a photographer for a few years. I did it to bring in some extra money. I had no passion for it. Not like I have for painting."

"And you worked mostly out of Barano in those years," Nonna Maria said.

"Yes," Pepe the Painter said. "I had a small studio a few meters from my home. This way, my wife and I would have all our meals together. But all that you already knew. Which means to me, you came sniffing around for something else."

"You heard about the woman whose body was found in Barano?" Nonna Maria said. "On the side of a road, no bag, nothing to tell us who she was and where she was from."

"Of course," Pepe the Painter said. "The body was found less than two kilometers from my house. The carabinieri have been up there night and day since, asking everyone if they knew this poor soul."

"I think I might know who she is," Nonna Maria said. "I'm not sure, and I've not even seen the body. But there's something about it that makes me think I know this woman. And if I'm right, then I think you know her as well."

Pepe the Painter rested the panino on a side table and put a hand on top of one of Nonna Maria's. "Do you have a name?" he asked.

Nonna Maria turned and looked at Pepe the Painter. "I think it might be Fernanda Matturana," she said.

Pepe the Painter stared at Nonna Maria for several moments. Then he slumped in his chair, leaned his head back, ran his hands over his thick strands of hair, and closed his eyes.

23.

"IT FEELS LIKE it happened a lifetime ago," Pepe the Painter said. "And yet, at the same time, as soon as you spoke her name, it's as if it were yesterday."

"Like most memories we keep buried," Nonna Maria said. "Both the good ones and the bad."

"I tried to help her back then," Pepe said. "I know you did as well. But you know how it is when you are young and in love. You listen only to what your heart tells you."

"She was in love with a married man," Nonna Maria said. "But that wasn't her biggest mistake. Her error was in trusting him and believing he was in love with her."

"Carlo brought a dark cloud to every door he passed," Pepe said. "He married a woman who treated him well enough. In return, what did she get out of the life they shared, the children she bore him, the home she took care of, the abuse she endured from his family? A man who chased any woman who caught his eye and gambled away every lira."

"Carlo's affairs were an open secret," Nonna Maria said. "He made no attempt to hide the many women he brought to a bed.

Not even from his wife. Except for Fernanda. That romance was kept under sealed lips."

"He had good reason for that," Pepe said. "He had been warned by her father on more than one occasion to stay clear of his daughter. If her father had so much as heard a rumor about the two of them, he would have come to Carlo's door looking to shed his blood."

"But the threat only made Carlo bolder," Nonna Maria said. "And he also knew what many of us did, that Fernanda's father was not well and did not have long to live."

"He never knew about their affair," Pepe said. "On his deathbed, he asked me to keep an eye on Fernanda. She was his youngest and his most vulnerable. That was his only request, Nonna Maria, all he asked of me after a friendship that began when we were both barely old enough to walk. And I failed to honor his wishes. I failed the man whose grave I cried over."

"It was a different time, Pepe," Nonna Maria said. "If Fernanda had stayed she would have brought shame to her family. There was nothing you could do to keep her on the island."

"I should have done everything in my power to keep her and her child together," Pepe said. "Not sit by and allow what happened to happen."

"Carlo's family had the means to buy silence," Nonna Maria said. "Back then his family controlled the fortunes of Barano. They decided Fernanda's future and the future of her child. They took advantage of her mother, fresh off having lost her husband, now faced with a scandal she could not bear. They convinced Fernanda and her family it was better for everyone involved if they took the child, claimed it as their own."

"Fernanda was sent to Naples before most of us knew she was pregnant," Pepe said. "I was told she had gone to university to study to be a pharmacist. Carlo sent his wife away as well, to live in Salerno with her family. It was a perfect ruse and I fell for it, like the fool I am."

"When did you know the truth?" Nonna Maria asked.

"I suspected something when Fernanda didn't return to Ischia at the end of her semester," Pepe said. "It was unlike her. She loved the island and would never stay away unless it was by force or threat."

"But Carlo's wife did come back to Ischia," Nonna Maria said. "With a newborn she claimed as her own."

"And Fernanda never set foot on Ischia again," Pepe said. "A sad tale in every respect."

"And it grows even sadder if Fernanda did return to see the child she was forced to leave behind," Nonna Maria said. "A child who is now a grown woman."

"Her name is Assunta," Pepe said. "As far as I know she has never been told the truth about her real mother. The only family she has known has been Carlo, his wife, and their children."

"Ischia is filled with secrets and gossip," Nonna Maria said. "The secrets are sealed as if buried under a mountain of rocks. The gossip spread by whispers from one set of ears to another."

Pepe nodded. "If the gossip has reached Assunta's ears she has given no sign," he said. "And I see her on occasion. She is kind enough to bring me fresh fruit and herbs from her garden. It pains me sometimes to look at her, knowing how much I failed her mother."

"Does she resemble Fernanda?" Nonna Maria asked.

Pepe stood up and reached behind him and scanned through a batch of framed portraits resting against the wall. He lifted one from the center and showed it to Nonna Maria. "As if they were twins," he said.

Nonna Maria took the framed portrait and held it with both hands. She stared at it and slowly shook her head, then she handed it back to Pepe. She stood, folded the chair and rested it against a side table. She then placed a hand on Pepe the Painter's shoulder.

"What do you plan to do?" he asked.

"First, I need to find out if the dead woman is indeed Fernanda," Nonna Maria said. "And if she is, then there is only one thing to do. Tell a young woman the truth."

"Anything you need, Nonna Maria," Pepe the Painter said. "Anything at all and I'll be there to help."

24.

CAPTAIN MURINO AND Nonna Maria stood outside the Bar Calise, their backs against a low stone wall. The bar, open all day every day regardless of season, was, as usual, filled to capacity. It stretches a full block, a brisk ten-minute walk from the port, and has been a meeting place for both young and old dating back to the early 1960s. It is noted for its excellent pastries and gelati and for a team of experienced waiters who do their best to avoid making eye contact.

This time of year, it was especially crowded due to the presence of Aldo Poli. He played the Bar Calise every summer, sitting on a perch above the dance floor, happily gazing around at the full house that came to hear him sing and play every night of the week. He began his sets at nine in the evening and wrapped up at three in the morning. He was tall, with a thick head of black hair and a crooner's voice. He always engaged in a friendly back-and-forth with the patrons, both locals and tourists. He would move easily from Neapolitan love ballads to contemporary tunes and sang his songs in three languages, including English and French.

"I came to see Aldo my very first night in Ischia," Captain

Murino said. "I knew no one, of course, and initially sat at a corner table, content to listen to the music and watch as the people reacted to the different songs he sang. On some, there were tears. On others, they sang along. And on others still, there was dancing. Not just on the dance floor, but between the tables."

"He loves his work," Nonna Maria said. "And that love is felt by those who come to hear him sing. It doesn't matter how old or young someone is, the right song can touch a special place in anyone's heart."

"Do you have a favorite song?" Captain Murino asked, glancing at Nonna Maria.

"Parla Mi D'Amore, Mariu," Nonna Maria said. "It's an old one. Even older than I am. But Aldo knows it and sings it with all his heart. I try to come by a few nights a week to hear him, and if he knows I'm here, he plays it for me."

"Why that song?" Captain Murino asked.

"It was the first song I danced to with my husband," Nonna Maria said. "We were both young, teenagers really. But it was during that first dance, we both knew we had found the one we wanted to spend the rest of our lives with. And each time I hear it, I think of him."

"Your husband was a lucky man, Nonna Maria," Captain Murino said. "I would have enjoyed watching the two of you dance to that particular song."

"I understand a young friend of mine came by to see you today," Nonna Maria said. "I hope you were able to calm his fears."

"I've never met a young man as nervous as Federico

Castagna," Captain Murino said. "You would think he was being sent to the gallows later in the day."

"He is the way he is with good reason," Nonna Maria said. "I sent him to see you because he drove down from Barano the night the woman was found on the side of the road. His car hit something, and he thought he might have hit and killed the woman."

"I assured him he did not hit anyone and was neither a suspect nor a witness," Captain Murino said. "I was going to offer him a coffee but I thought that might not be the best idea given his nervous condition."

"You freed him of his concerns," Nonna Maria said. "That was more than enough. He's a nice young man and takes good care of his loved ones. He doesn't need the weight of a crime on his shoulders."

"I wish it were that simple a case to solve," Captain Murino said. "In my six years on Ischia, this is by far the most difficult one I've had to confront."

"Even more difficult than the case of the stolen necklace?" Nonna Maria asked.

"I know you have your doubts about Signora Conte's accusation," Captain Murino said. "And you are not alone. The hotel staff feel as you do. As do a number of my men."

"And you, Captain?" Nonna Maria asked. "Do you believe Signora Conte?"

"It's an active investigation, Nonna Maria," Captain Murino said. "And still too early to know whether the necklace even exists. We'll get to the truth."

"Yes," Nonna Maria said. "We will."

"I know you will do all you can to prove Loretta's innocence," Captain Murino said. "All I ask is you keep me up to date on your findings. As you have many times in the past on other cases."

"As you will do with me," Nonna Maria said.

"For the moment, the case in Barano has a higher priority," Captain Murino said. "To date, we have not been able to identify the poor woman who was found dead on the road. The sooner we do, the easier it will be to track down the one who killed her."

"I may be of help to you with that," Nonna Maria said.

"Nonna Maria, if you know this woman, you must give me her name," Captain Murino said.

"I have a feeling I do," Nonna Maria said. "But it's just that. I haven't seen the woman or any photos of her body. Before I give you a name, I need to know for sure she is who I think it is."

"And if she is who you think?" Captain Murino asked.

"Then I will give you her name," Nonna Maria said. "And tell you the reason she returned to Ischia."

"If she were from Ischia wouldn't a family member have contacted us?" Captain Murino asked. "A friend, a classmate perhaps? There is an article about her death in the local paper. If she were from the island, someone would have known."

"If she is who I think, both her parents are dead," Nonna Maria said. "And her older brother and sister moved to the North long ago. Keep in mind, she's been gone from the island for more than twenty years. A memory fades with time."

"Why did she leave?"

"She was young and thought she was in love," Nonna Maria said. "And she was. But with the wrong man at the wrong time. A married man with a family of his own."

"And that would be reason enough to murder her decades later?" Captain Murino asked.

"Maybe not in places like Florence, where you were raised," Nonna Maria said. "But on an island like Ischia, and with the secrets this poor woman carried with her, then yes, it would be enough reason for someone to want her dead."

"And if you do indeed know this woman, would you also have an idea of who might have killed her?" Captain Murino asked.

Nonna Maria looked at Captain Murino, the booming voice of Aldo Poli echoing behind them, and nodded. "Yes, Captain," she said. "I would."

25.

NONNA MARIA WALKED the silent side streets of Ischia Ponte. It was late in the evening and she was far removed from the packed restaurants and clubs that lined the main boulevard of the neighborhood, filled at this hour with both tourists and locals enjoying the varied night life Ischia offered in the summer months. The dark, barren streets were separated from the high-end boutiques and bars by mere yards, but they might as well have been on another island, as far removed as they were in both appearance and financial standing. These side streets were among the poorest parts of the island.

The homes were built of stone, many of them small and in drastic need of repair, and each of them housed as many as three families. Most faced the lapping waters of the bay, the beaches used mainly by the locals and seldom ventured into by tourists. The residents made up the lower working class of Ischia, earning a meager living from the sea or as chambermaids and hotel servants, while a few got by selling trinkets to tourists, each one looking to take in enough money to get them not only through the summer but past the bleak fall and winter periods when the island was left to the locals.

Nonna Maria knew these streets as well as she knew the people who lived behind the shuttered windows. For many years she had lived among them, born and raised on Ischia Ponte. She could walk every curved path, the sandy stone steps and sharp inclines, limping past strewn garbage, lounging feral cats, and dark alleyways, making her way with a navigator's instincts.

She returned often to these streets, walking them under the cover of darkness, lost in thought and wrapped in the warm embrace of her childhood memories. Despite the poverty, even worse in the years she lived there, Nonna Maria had a fondness for the area and its people. They looked out for one another, a close-knit band that shared what little they had and seldom, if ever, complained.

The mornings were filled with song, as women hung laundry out to dry on clothing lines strung from rusty balconies or tied from one iron bar to another. They sang the Neapolitan ballads of their ancestors, many of the lyrics filled with tormented love and sadness for lives taken much too soon, sung with a passion that could only come from the voice of one who lived through those moments. Other songs were sung with joy and laughter, lyrics filled with sexual innuendo and lust, the women's hand gestures giving further expression to the words.

Nonna Maria's mother had married young, as many of the local girls did and even as she herself ended up doing. Her name was Graziella, but she was known to all as Gali. She was tall and slender, with rich brown hair and a pair of eyes that her father, Giovanni, often said "were the envy of the stars above."

Nonna Maria was one of six children, three older brothers and two younger sisters, and left school in fourth grade. She helped with the cooking and cleaning and, when she was old enough, was sent out to work in an uncle's grocery store.

If anyone in the neighborhood was ever in need of help or was looking for sound advice from a trusted friend, they always made their way to Gali. And she never once let them down.

It was a lesson not lost on Nonna Maria.

She turned a corner and began to make her way down a narrow alleyway. She was heading back home, her mind loaded down with the weight of the accusation against her goddaughter and the possible murder of a friend she had not seen for decades but had never forgotten.

It was a hot and humid night and she walked at a slow pace, her right hip causing her more pain than usual, the black tote bag she always carried filled with an array of fresh fruit she had purchased from the stand of an old friend. In the morning she planned to make a large fruit salad for three of her grandchildren who were expected for a visit. She would wait for their arrival and enlist their help in preparing the fruit salad, swearing them to secrecy as to what she did to make it such a delicious treat. After the fruit was cut, Nonna Maria would take out a large bowl and squeeze the juices from two large oranges and three lemons at the base. Then she tossed in the fruit and squeezed two more large oranges and three lemons on top of the massive mound of sliced and diced fruit. Then she tossed again and added six cubes of ice. As Nonna Maria would look at the happy faces of her grandchildren, she knew that one day long after she was no longer a part of their lives, they would prepare a fruit salad in the same manner.

"A woman should not be out at this hour of the night," a

man's voice said, coming at her from behind. "Especially one as old as you."

"I walk where I want, when I want," Nonna Maria said, not bothering to turn around. She did not recognize the voice but knew the accent was not from either a local or anyone from Naples.

"Maybe so," the man said, stepping closer. "But there is always a risk walking down dark streets this late in the evening."

"I have no idea what time it is," Nonna Maria said. "I don't own a watch."

The man was close enough now for Nonna Maria to feel his presence and smell the strong scent of his cologne. He put a thick hand on her shoulder and brought her to a halt. He turned her around and she stood facing him. He was a large man, thick around the chest, and was dressed in dark colors, clothes a bit too heavy for this time of year. He had black spectacles and a wide smile on his face. The two of them stood facing each other, Nonna Maria's back braced against a cold stone wall.

"Allow me a moment of your time," the man said. "What I have to say won't take very long."

"That's good," Nonna Maria said. "Especially when talking to someone as old as I am."

"You are putting yourself in a situation you have no business being in," the man said. "I'm here to tell you to bring it to a stop. I would hate to see you get hurt in any way."

"And you will be the one who will hurt me?" Nonna Maria asked.

The man squeezed the top of Nonna Maria's shoulder. She felt the sharp jolt of pain, but didn't betray it in her expression.

"If it comes to that, I will," he said. "And believe me, it wouldn't bother me a bit."

"I believe you," Nonna Maria said.

"So, go and be a sweet old lady and don't make me come back and look for you a second time," the man said, still holding the grip. "Forget about a necklace that doesn't even belong to you and worry about yourself."

The man then leaned down closer to Nonna Maria, his lips close to her left ear. "This is a sample of what will be done if you don't walk away from what doesn't concern you," he whispered.

The man stepped back and gripped Nonna Maria's shoulders with both hands and shoved her down to the stone pavement. He lifted his right leg, ready to land a hard blow to the center of her stomach.

The blow never reached its target.

The man felt an excruciating pain in the center of his back. A closed fist and a powerful punch sent him face-first against the stone wall.

Il Presidente looked down at Nonna Maria and helped her up. He then let go of her hand and spun the man around to face him. He landed two swift punches to the center of the man's chest, leaving him gasping for breath. The man doubled over and Il Presidente slammed his right knee against the center of the man's face, crushing his nose, sending blood spurting down his lips and staining the front of his dark blue shirt. Il Presidente steadied his feet on the slippery stones and readied himself to rain more blows on the stunned man.

"I've had enough excitement for tonight," Nonna Maria said,

gently placing a hand on the center of Il Presidente's back. "We both should be getting home."

Il Presidente turned and looked at Nonna Maria for a few moments and then nodded. He turned back to the man, grabbed him by his throat, and glared directly into his eyes. "You see me now?" he said. "Answer me. You see me now?"

"Yes," the man said with a bit of effort. "I see you."

"Good," Il Presidente said. "Because if you ever go near Nonna Maria again, the next time you see me, I will kill you."

Il Presidente then tossed the man against the stone wall, watching his head land with a low thud and his body sink slowly to the pavement.

Il Presidente turned to Nonna Maria and she put her right arm under his left elbow and they started to walk slowly out of the alleyway.

"You shouldn't be out around here this late at night," Nonna Maria said to him. "You don't know the streets the way I do. You never know who you could run into."

Il Presidente smiled. "I don't know what I was thinking," he said.

26.

NONNA MARIA SAT on a hard-backed wooden chair, staring up at the framed photo of her late husband, Gabriel. A blood-pressure monitor was attached to her right arm and a hot cup of coffee rested on the table. Her nephew, Agostino, stood over her, gauging her pressure, a frown creasing his forehead. "There are times, Zia, when I simply don't understand why you do the things you do," he said to her. He spoke in a calm and soothing voice, as was his manner, but beneath the surface simmered a deep-seated concern for the aunt he loved as much as his own mother.

"I went for a walk, Agostino," Nonna Maria said. "Nothing more than that."

"Yes, a walk," Agostino said, removing the blood-pressure wrap from around her arm. "Late at night, on dark side streets with no lights where the worst could have happened to you and almost did."

"It was nothing," she said. "Il Presidente brought you here for no reason. I feel fine. You must have many other patients that need your help more than I do."

"You have bruises on your shoulders and a gash on the side

113

of your face," Agostino said. "And, from what I've been told, I could be checking on you in the hospital instead of your dining room."

Agostino reached into his black medical bag and pulled out a large circular jar and placed it on the table. "What is that?" Nonna Maria asked.

"It's a cream for your bruises," Agostino said. "I'll rub some on before I leave and I would like it to be applied twice a day for five days. If you can manage to do it for yourself, fine. If not, I'll make sure your tenant downstairs comes up and rubs it on."

"I can do it myself," Nonna Maria said. "And Il Presidente is not my tenant. He's my friend."

"And a good friend he's proven to be, Zia," Agostino said. "If it weren't for him, that man might well have left you for dead."

Nonna Maria looked up at her nephew and rested a hand on top of his. "I know how much you worry about me," she said. "I'm sorry to have caused you such concern. Sit and have a cup of my coffee. It will help calm your nerves."

Agostino stared at Nonna Maria for a moment, then shook his head. "One cup," he said. "And I don't want it with three teaspoons of sugar, or a piece of chocolate, or a few drops of scotch. I don't have the stomach of a Viking like you."

Nonna Maria lifted the espresso pot from the tray in the center of the table, reached for a cup, filled it, and handed it to Agostino. He took the cup and made his way around the table, pulled back a chair and sat across from his aunt. He couldn't help but smile at her. "Your blood pressure is normal, as hard as it is for me to believe," he said. "And mine is probably much higher than it should be, thanks to hearing about your adventures."

"In so many ways, you remind me of him," Nonna Maria said, looking up at the framed photo of her husband, Gabriel. "He worried about me too. He was always afraid something would happen to me, an accident, an illness. As it turned out, he was the one who ended up with a sickness that took his life."

"He loved you, that's why he worried," Agostino said. He turned to glance up at the framed photo, taken when Gabriel was in his thirties. He was a handsome man with vivid eyes, a light brown mustache, and thinning hair. "Many years have passed since his death, but I know how much you still miss him."

"He's never left me, Agostino," Nonna Maria said. "He's where he's always been. In my heart."

Agostino sipped his coffee, then opened a leather-bound notebook, pulled a pen from his shirt pocket and scribbled down a few notes. Nonna Maria stared at her nephew and smiled. "Are you writing about me?" she asked.

"A few reminders for the next time I come," he said. "There are some vitamins I would like you to take. Help you keep your strength up since I doubt you are eating as well as you should and you only drink coffee and white wine."

"What else is there to drink?" Nonna Maria asked.

Agostino shook his head. "For you, nothing I could think of at the moment," he said.

Nonna Maria looked across the table at her nephew and thought back to the time he first left the island to attend medical school in the North. He was a gifted student and it was clear his services would be much in demand. After he completed his residency in Bologna, he was besieged with job offers from the best hospitals in Italy and could have named his price at any of them. Instead, he rebuffed all offers and chose to return to Ischia and care for the people he knew and loved.

That was nearly thirty years ago, and in that time he had built a large and successful practice, dutifully making house calls, catering to the locals and the occasional tourist who fell ill during their stay on the island. He had a family of his own now as well, having married his high school love and together raised three sons and a daughter, two of the four children now in medical school in Naples.

He was a handsome man, his brown hair touched with gray at the temples, and though he wore glasses, they always seemed to be hanging off a chain around his neck. He had deep brown eyes and never raised his voice. He ran five miles every morning before sunup through the pine gardens near the Bar Calise and had a glass of Fernet-Branca every night before heading off to bed.

Agostino put his pen back in his shirt pocket, closed his notebook and dropped it into his medical bag. He finished his coffee and pushed his chair back. "There are two large bags in the kitchen for you to take home," Nonna Maria said. "I made a few loaves of zucchini bread and some red peppers with olives and capers. And I didn't forget the stuffed mushrooms you like so much and a container of eggplant parmigiana. That one is for your little one, Guido. He reminds me of you when you were a boy, always looking for a fresh eggplant parmigiana."

"When do you find time to do all this cooking?" Agostino asked. "From what I hear, you are always out and about, looking into one thing or another."

"Never believe what you hear," Nonna Maria said. "And I didn't cook anything. My stove does all the work."

"I'll be back to see you at the end of the week," Agostino said. "I hope you can stay out of trouble until then. And don't forget to put that cream on your bruises. As a favor to me, if nothing else."

"I promise," Nonna Maria said. "If only I can ask a favor in return."

"Name it," Agostino said.

"I need to see some medical records," Nonna Maria said. "They would be in one of the hospitals in Naples. A hospital that would have been around twenty or so years ago. Do they keep records that far back?"

"If they're worth keeping," Agostino said. "They should all be logged into the computer system. What exactly would I be looking for?"

"A baby's birth," Nonna Maria said. "The name given to the child and the names listed as the mother and father."

"I need a name, Zia," Agostino said. "I won't be able to find anything without a name."

"All I can give you is the mother's name," Nonna Maria said. "I hope that will be enough for you to find what I need."

"It's a place to start," Agostino said. "What's the woman's name?"

"Her name was Fernanda Matturana," Nonna Maria said.

27.

FEDERICA D'AMATO PARKED her black Vespa against the white stone wall of the medical examiner's office. She took off her helmet and placed it in the rear compartment. The street was quiet, the stores and shops shuttered for the long afternoon respite. Federica was dressed in a crisp white blouse, short blue skirt, and blue Nike sneakers. She was in her mid-thirties, her long brown hair masking a thin and tanned face. She had been Ischia's medical examiner for the past three years, transferred to the island after working in a small town in Sicily, on the outskirts of Palermo, for four years. She was the youngest of five children born to a Sicilian doctor and his wife, a nurse from Reggio Calabria. From the youngest age, Federica had been fascinated with the world of medicine, encouraged by both parents to pursue her interest. She devoured books on anatomy and excelled in all her classes. While her parents would have preferred her to choose a different branch of medicine, Federica was determined to become a medical examiner, making her one of the few women in Italy to work in that field.

She had seen quite a number of butchered bodies in her time working in Sicily, but her years on Ischia had been relatively calm by comparison. The death of a tour boat captain the previous year had caused a bit of a stir, but otherwise there had been few bodies to challenge her abilities, their deaths resulting mostly from disease or natural occurrence. That held true until she had the woman whose body was found on the streets of Barano on her morgue slab. Her death was the most violent she had yet encountered on the island.

Federica was walking toward the front door of the medical examiner's office, a key in her right hand, when she turned and saw Nonna Maria heading toward her, moving slowly under the glare of a blazing sun.

"You shouldn't be out in this heat, Nonna Maria," Federica said to her as she drew closer. "It's not good for you."

"So everyone tells me," Nonna Maria said. "But I have always liked the quiet this time of day, and I don't mind the heat."

"And I have learned it is best not to try to talk you out of doing what you like to do," Federica said.

"What I would like to do is talk to you about the dead woman found in Barano," Nonna Maria said.

"I'm sorry, Nonna Maria," Federica said. "There's not much I'm allowed to tell you. I examined her body and sent my report on to the carabinieri. It's an active investigation and I can't give out any details."

"She may have been a friend of mine," Nonna Maria said. "From years ago. But I'm still not certain. If she is, then I think I can help Captain Murino find out who killed her."

Federica leaned against the wall of the medical examiner's building and looked over at Nonna Maria. "Well, by now you've heard talk of how she died," she said. "Even some of the tourists seem to know she was strangled. I am always amazed at how interested people get when it comes to death, especially a sudden and violent one."

"Maybe because we live in quiet fear of our own," Nonna Maria said. "Are you allowed to tell me what she looked like?"

Federica shrugged. "I don't see why that would be crossing any boundaries," she said. "She was tall, slender, dark skin, darker hair. She looked older than I think she was. There were many scrapes and bruises on her body. Some of them fresh, from the incident. But others were older, slower to heal."

"How old would you say she was?" Nonna Maria asked.

"Hard to tell for certain," Federica said. "But if I had to pin it down, I would say she would be in her early forties. Though, as I said, the wear and tear on her body made her appear older."

"She must have lived a hard life," Nonna Maria said. "And probably not by choice or design."

"A worker's life," Federica said. "There were deep-set marks on her knees, and her hands were calloused and worn. Her feet were rough-edged and the cut of her hair was uneven, as if she did it herself."

"As most women short on money and time do," Nonna Maria said.

"Other than that, and the scar on one side of her face, there isn't much else I can add, Nonna Maria," Federica said.

"Tell me about the scar," Nonna Maria said.

"It was old, nearly vanished," Federica said. "If it weren't for her tan skin, it would have hardly been noticeable. It was ragged and showed some tear. A bite of some sort."

"A dog bite," Nonna Maria said. "She was bitten when she

was eight years old. We were taking a shortcut across a large farm when a dog appeared out of nowhere. He jumped at my friend, who was closer to him, and bit her on the face. With all the blood that ran down her cheek and her screams, I thought for sure the dog had taken her eye."

Federica reached out and placed a hand on Nonna Maria's arm. "It did have all the markings of a dog bite," she said. "A bite from many years ago. So, then, you do know this woman?"

"Yes," Nonna Maria said. "I do know her, and we can now put a name to the body."

"Having her name helps, no doubt," Federica said. "But there's still a killer out there whose name we don't know."

"Someone knows the name," Nonna Maria said. "And you have made it easier for that someone to be found."

28.

NONNA MARIA SAT on the stone bench in front of Saint Peter's Church, casually gazing out at the throngs of passing tourists. She needed a distraction from the discovery she had made only hours earlier. And it gave her a small amount of pleasure to see the colorful and expensive ensembles the tourists chose to wear, especially the women, for their nightly excursions. She never quite grasped why anyone needed to get dressed up in their finest simply to enjoy a walk or dinner at any of the restaurants of the island. With the exception of the dining rooms in the five-star hotels, where men were required to wear a jacket, there were no dress codes. Ischia was a place where everyone was accepted as they were and what they wore made little, if any, impression on the locals.

She saw two of her daughters, Francesca and Nunzia, turn a corner and head toward her, both walking at a brisk pace. Nonna Maria smiled as they made their way to the stone bench. Francesca, the older of the two, sat down, while Nunzia stood facing her mother, her back to the passing tourists.

"Did you get the roasted chickens I had Pietro send you earlier?" Nonna Maria asked.

Francesca nodded. "We had them for lunch, along with a to-mato, red onion, and basil salad," she said. "Pietro is a master at what he does. He was kind enough to give me his recipe two years back, but I still haven't managed to make them taste as delicious as he does."

"It's the wood he uses," Nonna Maria said. "He doesn't buy local. He has his wood shipped to him from somewhere in the North. The smoke from the wood gives the chicken that extra touch of flavor."

Nunzia quietly paced back and forth, her pretty face shrouded with a look of concern. She was the daughter who most resembled Nonna Maria physically but not in manner. She was better educated than her other siblings, read a wide range of books, from thrillers to biographies to historical fiction, and had a finely tuned business sense. She and her husband, an ac-countant who worked for a large firm in Naples, had invested wisely and owned four apartments in the port area. They lived in one with their two children and counted on the other three for rental income. But even now that Nunzia was a woman in her late forties, with a loving family of her own, Nonna Maria always felt Nunzia was the most vulnerable of her children. She thought her daughter too quick to worry, anticipating the worst in any situation.

Francesca, her oldest, on the other hand, was fearless and headstrong. She wasn't afraid to speak her mind and voice her opinion on any subject, quick to argue and make a strong de-fense of her case. But she was even quicker to laugh and seemed to take pleasure from every moment of life that she could. She had her father's good heart, donating clothes and handing out gifts to those less fortunate than she was, and could always be counted on to lend someone in need a helping hand, be it through a loan to start a business or simply by sitting with them and helping to find a solution to their problems.

Francesca and her husband prospered, as many others in Ischia had, working the tourist trade. Along with her brothers, Mario and Joseph, they owned a fleet of taxis, buses, and boats that took tourists to their hotels, on tours of the island, and to various off-island destinations, from Capri to Procida to Positano. They, along with their other siblings, invested early in two of Ischia's prime hotels and watched them grow through the years from two stars to their current five-star status. When her brothers and her husband, Franco, first started their tourist business, it was Francesca who manned the phones, taking down reservations and booking tours, working from her kitchen table, armed only with a legal pad and a sharp pencil. Today, the company has a three-thousand-square-foot office occupying two floors of a small building in the main area of the port, and employs a staff of one hundred and twenty-five, working out of Ischia, Naples, and Procida. Francesca's only child, Arturo, helps manage the staff from an office in Molo Beverello in Naples.

"Maybe you should sit here between me and your sister," Nonna Maria said to Nunzia. "And then, instead of moving back and forth, you can tell me what it is that seems to be troubling you."

"I don't want to sit," Nunzia said. "And what's troubling me, and Francesca as well, is that you could have been hurt or, even worse, killed the other night. It's only by the grace of God that a tragedy didn't happen."

"Maybe, more by the grace of Il Presidente," Nonna Maria said. "But since I'm sitting in front of a church, let God take the credit."

"It's easy to joke about now, Mama," Francesca said. "But if the worst had happened, we would have been inside the church a few hours ago, sitting through your funeral mass."

"But the worst didn't happen," Nonna Maria said. "Which only means you will have to wait a while longer to sit through my funeral mass."

"It is both foolish and dangerous for you to keep putting yourself in these situations," Nunzia said. "And for the life of me, I don't understand why you do. And I never have."

"We know you want to be there for your friends when they're in trouble," Francesca said. "And you always have, and it is one of the many reasons so many on this island love and respect you. But we worry about the dangers you put yourself in. You were lucky Il Presidente showed up when he did. But, come the next time, what if he isn't there to protect you?"

Nonna Maria looked at both her daughters and nodded. "You worry about me because you love me," she said. "And daughters should worry about their mothers, it's only natural. Especially as we get on in years. But I'm too old to change my ways. I understand your concern. When I was around your age, I worried about my mother, your grandmother. She went her own way, regardless. And her way was a lot more dangerous than anything I've ever done."

"Because of the war," Francesca said.

"Because of the war, yes," Nonna Maria said. "Along with all the fears and horrors it brought with it."

"That was a different time," Nunzia said. "The island was under attack and then occupied by the Nazis. She had to take risks. She had no other choice."

Nonna Maria stood and faced her daughters. "There's always a choice," she said. "Back then during the war and now. You can choose to help, or you can choose to stand by and do nothing. Now, walk with me to my house. We can talk on the way, and once we're there, and if you still feel like talking, we'll do it over a bottle of cold wine."

Together they walked from the stone bench of Saint Peter's, turned the corner, and made their way to Nonna Maria's house, Nonna Maria walking between them, a hand resting under each daughter's folded arm.

29.

"ISCHIA WAS GETTING bombed almost every night," Nonna Maria said. "My mother was told, along with my aunts and uncles, to run for the nearest shelter as soon as they heard the air raid siren. They were all so young and so afraid, with good reason. They had seen many on the island die from the bombs and they had suffered a loss of their own—a brother, my uncle John, was killed by the British when he was not even twenty years old."

"I can't even imagine what it must have been like to live like that, day to day," Nunzia said.

"No one really can," Nonna Maria said. "Not unless you've lived through it and seen it all with your own eyes. The lack of food was as much of a problem as the bombings, and drinking water was in short supply. You need a special kind of courage to survive years living as they were forced to live."

"I used to ask Nonna all the time to tell us about the years here during the war," Francesca said. "But she never liked to talk about it."

"Few of the ones who survived did," Nonna Maria said. "It was their way of dealing with the horror they lived through. For them, it was better to leave their memories buried, along with the loved ones who were lost."

"But you know all the stories," Nunzia said. "Or at least most of them."

"When they got together, usually over coffee or a few bottles of wine, they would talk among themselves about those years," Nonna Maria said. "And I would sit in a quiet corner and do what I do best: listen."

"They probably thought you weren't paying attention," Francesca said with a smile. "Little did they know."

"They always spoke in low voices," Nonna Maria said. "Their words were filled with a pain and a sense of loss I had never heard before from adults. Many of them shed tears as they talked. I remember every story I heard, but there was one above all the others that had an effect on me. I can't explain why it has stayed with me all these years. Maybe it was because the one telling the story was my mother."

Francesca looked over at Nunzia, both with surprised looks on their faces. Their mother seldom spoke of the troubles her own mother and father had endured during the war, losing a son, a grandson, a son-in-law, and three nephews. She didn't often mention the difficult years after the war, when food and milk were scarce and the drinking water smelled of burnt rubber. Whatever fears those postwar years had inflicted were lodged deep within Nonna Maria and she chose, for the most part, to keep them buried, known only to herself.

"What did she tell you?" Francesca asked, hoping to take advantage of one of the rare occasions her mother seemed willing to speak about a part of her life that had been safely locked away.

They were near the front landing of Nonna Maria's house and she reached for the black iron railing and leaned her back against it. "The bombs usually fell at night," she said to her daughters. "At first it was Nazi planes that dropped their shells, and then came the Americans, sometimes even the British. It didn't really matter who was dropping them. What mattered was that our people were dying."

"I'm so glad you were at least spared having to live through that," Nunzia said.

"I was born five years after the war's end," Nonna Maria said. "But the ones who survived were never the same, even my parents. There were pieces of them that those years had torn away and nothing could ever make them whole again. My mother most of all."

"Was she injured in one of the bombing raids?" Francesca asked.

Nonna Maria stared at her daughters in silence for a few moments, her mind filled with dark images from years past and frightful stories once told never to be forgotten. "It was a summer day, warm and humid, much like today," she said, her voice soft and low. "My mother and two of her brothers were coming from a walk on the beach, walking back toward the house. The boys were running and hiding among the rubble, making a game of it. My mother let them run loose, watching them play, hearing them laugh. That was a rare sound during those years."

"The war stripped them of their childhood," Nunzia said. "It's what Uncle Claudio used to always tell me."

Nonna Maria nodded. "They were no more than a ten-minute walk from home when the air raid siren sounded," she said. "My mother gathered her brothers, held their hands as tight as she could, and then the three began to run. My mother was determined to get them both home alive. They were in bare feet and ran as fast as they could, and it looked as if they would make it. Then a bomb landed down the road from where they were and the force tossed them to the ground. They lay there stunned and covered in dust for what they thought was a long time, but was probably no more than a few seconds."

"Were they injured?" Francesca asked.

"They had cuts and scrapes from the blast," Nonna Maria said. "And the boys had trouble swallowing, their mouths filled with dust and debris. But when my mother looked down, she realized she was bleeding from a deep cut on her stomach. She was wearing a blue shirt and soon it was drenched in blood. She tried to stand but felt light-headed and shaky on her feet."

"Were they able to call for help?" Nunzia asked.

"The streets were abandoned," Nonna Maria said. "Even if they had cried out there would have been no one to hear them. Instead, her two brothers, so young, so innocent, each put one arm around my mother, lifted her to her feet, and began to drag her toward their home."

"They couldn't have been more than seven or eight years old," Francesca said.

"They weren't," Nonna Maria said. "But they dragged my

mother through smoke, fire, and haze, pulling with all their strength, all three soaked through with sweat and surrounded by the thick dust caused by the bomb."

"Was the rest of the family hiding in the basement shelter?" Nunzia asked.

"The other children were," Nonna Maria said. "But their mother and father were out looking for them, separated by the thick mounds of fallen stones caused by the bomb that fell. They both tossed aside large chunks of what had once been someone's home, calling out the names of my mother and her brothers."

Francesca rested a hand on Nonna Maria's arm and leaned closer to her. She caught the gleam of tears in her mother's eyes and the sadness etched now in her voice. "You've told us enough for one night, Mama," she said. "You should go up and get some rest. You can finish the story another time."

"I'll rest enough when I'm dead," Nonna Maria said. "And this is something you need to hear. It will tell you as much about me as it does about them."

"Let her finish," Nunzia said, brushing aside tears of her own.

"My mother's wound was causing her a great deal of pain, and even with the help of her brothers, they were moving slowly, finding it difficult to climb over the mounds of stone and rocks that blocked their path," Nonna Maria said. "They were tired, thirsty, and scared. My mother fell to her knees and leaned against a low wall, trying to catch her breath. She kept one hand pressed tight on her stomach, blood streaming through her fingers. She told her brothers to make their way home before the next bombs fell. She needed them to be safe. She would wait by the wall for them and trust them to send help soon as they could."

"Did they leave her?" Francesca asked.

"My mother gave them no other choice," Nonna Maria said. "And it was the right decision. The boys could move faster without her, able to climb over rocks and stones and make their way to safer ground. They hesitated at first, but at my mother's urging, they wrapped their arms around her, kissed her, turned, and ran toward their home. But first both brothers took off their soiled shirts, folded them, and pressed them tightly against my mother's stomach wound."

"She had to think she was going to die," Francesca said.

Nonna Maria slowly shook her head. "She knew her brothers would find their way to safety," she said. "That was all that mattered to her. She rested her head against the rock wall and closed her eyes. Despite the heavy heat of the day, her body was coated in a cold sweat and she shivered with each breath she took. Her eyes were heavy and burned from the smoke. She lay there for the longest time, every second inching closer to death, wondering if she would ever see her family again."

"How soon before they found her?" Nunzia asked.

"It took a few hours," Nonna Maria said. "Hours that must have felt like days to my mother. You lose sense of time in those moments. But her mother and father, helped by a number of friends, tossed aside the rocks and stones and cleared a path and made their way to my mother, her two brothers serving as their guide. She had saved their lives, and now it was their turn to save hers."

"She must have been so happy to see them," Francesca said.

"She was out cold by the time they got to her," Nonna Maria said. "Her father carried her home and someone went to find the pharmacist."

"You mean the doctor," Nunzia said.

"The doctor had died in an earlier bombing raid," Nonna Maria said. "The pharmacist was the closest thing there was to medical help during those years. She had lost a lot of blood and her lungs were congested. She developed a fever and there was no controlling the sweat soaking her body. She was in bed for three days before she opened her eyes. And a few days after that, she was able to sit up and eat some food and drink some coffee."

"She was lucky the wound didn't kill her," Francesca said.

"She was lucky the pharmacist knew what he was doing," Nonna Maria said. "He cleansed the wound and with very shaky hands sewed it up and bandaged it. All that remained years later was the scar."

"And that was the story you heard her tell?" Nunzia asked. "The one that has stayed with you all these years?"

"It explained the nightmares," Nonna Maria said. "There were many nights when my mother would wake from a deep sleep and scream for her brothers to run, to get to safety, to get home. She would be shouting about all the blood and how she couldn't make it stop. I would hear it from my bed, we all did, but I never knew the reason for those horrible dreams. Not until the night I heard her tell the story I just told you."

"Why did you tell us?" Francesca asked. "You don't like talking about those times. But tonight you made a point of telling us. Why?"

Nonna Maria looked at both her daughters and caressed their faces. "I want you to stop worrying about me," she said. "My mother survived that day and other days even worse. She didn't let anything stop her from protecting her family and helping her friends. So, if your Nonna could live through a war and bombings and a stomach wound that would have killed most people, then it is nothing for me to go for a late-night walk on the very streets where those bombs fell."

"To help your friends and protect your family?" Nunzia said.

"And to remember the ones who came before me and did the same," Nonna Maria said.

30.

NONNA MARIA WALKED the stone pathway through the gardens of the Excelsior Hotel, the manager, Antonio, by her side. "I cannot tell you how much this situation with Loretta has troubled me, Nonna Maria," he said. He spoke in a low voice, his manner, as ever, gentle and kind. "I have not slept since I first was told and will not sleep again until the matter is settled."

"Signora Conte remains a guest of the hotel," Nonna Maria said. "A free guest. At least, that's what I have heard."

"It was not my choice, Nonna Maria," Antonio said. "It's at the discretion of the owner, who thought it best that we protect the reputation of the hotel and keep the news out of the local papers. And, to this point, that much we have been able to accomplish."

"You don't need a local paper on this island to get your news, Antonio," Nonna Maria said. "All you need to do is open your front door or kitchen window. In less time than it takes to pour a cup of coffee, you will have heard all the news you need to hear."

They turned a corner and stood on a well-kept patio overlooking the pool and the back of the four-story hotel. There was a table in a corner with four soft chairs spread around it, and Antonio gestured toward it. "Let's sit in the shade for a bit, Nonna Maria," he said. "I find the heat this time of year drains all my strength. And, unlike the locals, I can't take the time for a three-hour afternoon nap."

Nonna Maria sat in a cushioned chair, her back to the pool, covered from the heat by the fronds of an overhanging palm. Antonio sat across from her. "I know better than to offer you anything to eat or drink," he said. "But if there is anything I can get for you, just say the word."

"Does Signora Conte spend most of her time in her room?" Nonna Maria said. "Or on the grounds of the hotel?"

"For the most part, in her room," Antonio said. "She goes out in the evening, around eight or so, and usually returns about midnight."

"And she allows your staff to clean her room?" Nonna Maria asked.

Antonio nodded. "She has not interfered with any of the work that needs to be done," he said. "She's kept her distance, makes her frustrations known to one and all, and is waiting, as we all are, for the carabinieri to bring their investigation to an end."

Nonna Maria reached down, lifted her black tote bag, and rested it on her knees. "I brought you something to eat," she said. "You are much too thin, and Southern Italian men can't allow themselves to be too thin."

"And why is that?" Antonio asked, smiling.

"Because then you look sinister," Nonna Maria said, returning the smile. She reached into her bag and took out a large panino wrapped in brown paper and several sealed containers. "I made breaded chicken and roasted peppers and broccoli rabe for the panino," she said. "And sautéed escarole and marinated mushrooms and a small green salad to go with it. I brought along a bottle of wine, but I know you never drink while on duty. So, that you can save for later."

"That is very kind of you, as always, Nonna Maria," Antonio said, sliding the panino from its wrapping. "But I should tell you, I don't drink wine whether on duty or off."

Nonna Maria looked at him for a moment. "No wine at all?" she asked, not bothering to hide the surprise in her voice.

"Not a drop," Antonio said. "My doctor in Naples tells me it would be better for my health in the long run."

"That doctor in Naples is wrong," Nonna Maria said. "You should go see my nephew Agostino. He would never tell you to stop drinking wine. And if he ever did, then keep looking for a doctor until you find one that tells you to enjoy a cold glass of D'Ambra white. That's when you'll know you found the one who cares about your health, in the long run and in the short."

Antonio took a bite of the panino. "This is so delicious," he said. "If we could serve panini like this in our restaurant, our hotel would always be filled with guests."

"You have an excellent chef," Nonna Maria said. "I hear she's one of the best cooks on the island."

"I would have you sample one of her excellent dishes, but I know better than to ask that," Antonio said.

"I am loyal to my stove," Nonna Maria said. "In over fifty years, she has never failed me."

Antonio rested the panino on the folded paper, wiped his

mouth with one of the paper napkins Nonna Maria had piled inside the wrapping, and sat back. "We are all sorry about the current situation," he said. "The staff feel terrible and helpless. But there is nothing to be done until the carabinieri find Signora Conte's necklace."

"What if a necklace were to be found?" Nonna Maria said. "Returned to Signora Conte's room, in the exact spot where she claims to have last seen it?"

"You have something in mind," Antonio said. "I have known you since I was a child and have heard more than enough stories to believe that Signora Conte has met her match when paired against you."

"She's a signora with money and connections," Nonna Maria said. "I'm nothing more than an old island woman looking to prove her goddaughter's claim of innocence."

"And how would an old island woman know how to find a necklace such as the one described by Signora Conte?" Antonio asked.

"On her own, it would not be possible," Nonna Maria said. "But if she had a friend in the business of buying and selling such items, she might be able to find one."

"But from what I've heard, you don't believe Signora Conte ever had a necklace," Antonio said. "If one were to suddenly appear, would that not prove she was telling the truth?"

"Signora Conte is a smart woman," Nonna Maria said. "She knows a necklace must be found, otherwise her story rests on a weak foundation. I would guess she has already made plans to have one placed near where Loretta had kept her things. Does your staff not have a place where they change into their uniforms?"

Antonio nodded. "A room in the basement, near the gym," he said. "They change there, have their coffee, even lunch if they so choose. It's out of sight of the guests, allowing them a few moments of privacy."

"And a perfect place to leave a necklace that the owner claims has been stolen by a member of that staff," Nonna Maria said.

"But you proposed to place a necklace back in Signora Conte's room," Antonio said.

"We are two mice chasing one piece of cheese," Nonna Maria said. "Two necklaces found when only one was claimed to be stolen. She can only choose one as the missing one."

"What do you need me to do?" Antonio asked.

Nonna Maria reached into her black tote bag and pulled out a red leather pouch tied with a blue ribbon. "Hold on to this for me," she said. "It is a necklace of rare value, loaned to me by an old friend. When the right moment presents itself, have it placed in Signora Conte's room. From what I've been told, it is worth twice the value of the one she claims was stolen."

"And what if you are correct and Signora Conte will have a necklace placed in the workers' lounge?" Antonio asked.

"It won't be worth as much as the one that will be placed in her room," Nonna Maria said. "It forces her to make a choice. Claim the one in her room as the one she says was stolen or choose the less expensive one found in the lounge. Prove that a crime has taken place or leave with a valuable necklace that is not hers. Which makes her either a liar or a thief."

"You said your friend lent you this expensive necklace," Antonio said. "May I ask where he got it?"

Nonna Maria stood, picked up her black tote and hung it over her right shoulder. "It was given to him by a friend in Rome," she said. "The necklace in your hands belongs to the Baroness Di Meglio."

Antonio looked down at the pouch he held in the palm of his right hand. "If it belongs to the Baroness it must be worth quite a bit," Antonio said. "Have much more value than the one Signora Conte claims was taken from her room."

"The trap has been put in place," Nonna Maria said. "Now we wait and see if Signora Conte takes the bait."

31.

THE CINEMA EXCELSIOR was filled to capacity, the first showing of the evening always drawing the largest crowd. Nonna
Maria sat in an aisle seat in the center of the small movie theater,
her black tote bag resting on her lap. It was her first time in the
theater, the first time she had ever been in a movie house of
any kind. She had walked past the theater hundreds of times but
never once felt the inclination to purchase a ticket and sit for two
hours and watch a movie.

A middle-aged woman sitting across the aisle from Nonna
Maria looked over at her and smiled. "I have been waiting
months to see this movie," she said. "I was the first in line,
waited for over an hour for the ticket window to open. Can't
wait until it begins. I can't remember the last time I was this
excited. How about you?"

Nonna Maria returned the smile. "I'm old," she said. "I don't
get excited. My nephew the doctor tells me it's not good for my
health."

Nonna Maria recognized the young woman as soon as she
saw her walk down the center aisle of the theater. She looked
to be in her early twenties and was dressed in a sleeveless black

dress and black sandals; her thick dark hair hung down the sides of her face and rested on the nape of her neck. She held on tight to the hand of a small child walking gingerly by her side, her eyes scanning the theater for any available seats.

Nonna Maria stood as the young woman approached her aisle. "You can have my seat, if you like," she said to her. "You can put the child on your lap and you can watch the movie together."

"That's very kind of you to offer," the young woman said. "But I couldn't take your seat. You should sit and enjoy the movie. I'll manage to find a place for me and my daughter."

"I'm not staying for the movie," Nonna Maria said. "It's not why I came. So, if you and your child don't take my seat, someone else will come along who will be more than happy to take it."

"If you didn't come to see the movie, why did you bother coming to the cinema?" the young woman asked.

"I came to see you," Nonna Maria said. "I need to talk to you."

"Talk to me about what?" the young woman asked.

Nonna Maria looked down at the child leaning against her mother's leg, one hand clutching the fabric of her dress. "There's no need to disappoint your daughter," she said. "Let her enjoy the movie. I'll wait for you both outside when it lets out. We can talk then."

"Have we met before?" the young woman asked. "I feel as if we have."

"A long time ago," Nonna Maria said. "You were just a few years older than your daughter. And we only glanced at each other from a distance. You looked like someone I once knew

142

and I stopped to get a closer look. It couldn't have lasted more than a minute."

"And did I?" the young woman asked. "Did I look like the person you once knew?"

Nonna Maria nodded. "Back then you did," she said. "And you do even more so now."

"And who is this woman?" she asked.

"She was my friend," Nonna Maria said. "And she was your mother."

The two women stared at each other for several moments and then Nonna Maria turned and walked out of the crowded cinema.

32.

GIOVANNI PARKED HIS taxi-van directly across the street from the Cinema Excelsior. He sat behind the wheel and waited as Nonna Maria approached the driver's side. "Do you want to sit inside?" he asked. "I have the air conditioner on. It will keep you cool. It's much too hot to be standing under this broiling sun."

"The inside of the theater was air-conditioned," Nonna Maria said. "In there it's as cold as the middle of January. I need the hot sun to warm me."

"I stopped by your nephew's medical studio as you asked," Giovanni said. "He was out on his rounds. But he left an envelope with your name on it to be given to me."

Giovanni reached across the front seat of his van, grabbed a sealed manila envelope, and handed it to Nonna Maria. She turned the envelope over, unclasped it, and pulled out the three stapled sheets of white paper resting inside. She handed the papers to Giovanni. "I can't see well with the sun at my back," Nonna Maria said. "Can you read for me? Not all the pages. Just the names of the birth mother and father and the doctor who signed the certificate."

Giovanni reached down into the console and grabbed a pair of wire-framed reading glasses. He carefully put them on, resting the pages on the steering wheel. He scanned the first page until he saw the names Nonna Maria had asked to hear. "The mother is listed as Fernanda Matturana," he said.

Nonna Maria closed her eyes and nodded. "And the father?"

"Carlo Trippiano," Giovanni said.

"Does it give any other information about them?" Nonna Maria asked.

"Matturana gave birth to a baby girl," Giovanni said. "Born in good health and without complications."

"What name did they give the baby?"

"Assunta," Giovanni said.

"Anything else?"

"It gives the ages of both the mother and the father," Giovanni said. "Carlo is listed as forty-five years of age and Fernanda as twenty-four, but there is a star next to her name."

"What does that mean?"

Giovanni looked farther down the page and then paused, turning to face Nonna Maria. "It says Fernanda died giving birth. It is written out a few lines below their names and ages."

Nonna Maria leaned against the driver's side door, the sun above starting to make its descent on the horizon, covering her in a mixture of light and shade. "The name of the doctor," she said. "It should be on the last page, or if not there, then at the bottom of the first."

Giovanni flipped the pages, running a finger along the written lines. "Here it is," he said. "The signature is scrawled but under that the name it is written out. Dr. Salvatore Almonte."

Nonna Maria stayed silent for a moment, staring across the street at the closed doors of the Cinema Excelsior. "I know I asked a lot of you today, Giovanni," she said. "But can I trouble you for one more favor?"

"Anything, Nonna Maria," Giovanni said. "For you it is never a bother, always a pleasure."

"Put those papers back in the envelope and take them to the carabinieri office," she said. "And hand them to Captain Murino."

"Of course," Giovanni said. "Do you need me to tell him anything?"

"Tell him I know who the woman found dead on the road in Barano is," Nonna Maria said. "And that I might also know who killed her."

Giovanni stared at Nonna Maria and then looked back at the papers he held in his hands. "You knew these people?" he asked.

Nonna Maria nodded. "And I should have been there to help one of them," she said. "But I failed to help my friend when she needed me."

"The mother who died during childbirth," Giovanni said.

"The mother those papers say died during childbirth," Nonna Maria said. "In so many ways, it's not a total lie. A part of her must have died that day. And every day after."

Nonna Maria rested a hand on Giovanni's arm and then turned and crossed the street, standing alone in the shade of the Cinema Excelsior.

33.

ARIANNA CONTE SAT on the patio of the Grand Hotel Excelsior, across from Antonio and Captain Murino. There was a half-eaten cornet on the center of a small plate resting to her left, alongside a large and now-cold cup of cappuccino, its white foam dissipated. She had gone for a morning swim and had been resting on a lounge chair by the extended private dock reserved for hotel guests, her arms, face, legs, and neck coated with coconut sunscreen. She had been planning yet another leisurely day, enjoying the free meals and extras that came with a stay at a five-star hotel, when she was approached by a beach attendant and told that the hotel manager and the captain of the carabinieri were waiting to see her on the patio.

She put on a green robe, decorated with an array of red flowers, and a pair of sandals that had a white pearl attached to the center. She made her way past the beach and up the stairs, crossed the street, and waited as the private gate buzzer clicked open the door and allowed her into the rear of the hotel grounds. She walked without haste, her mind racing with the numerous reasons they might want to speak to her, wondering if her reluctant partner had at last completed his task. A task that would clearly point the finger of guilt at the young chambermaid and eliminate any doubts as to the veracity of Arianna's story.

"What are you telling me?" she said, directing the question more to the captain than to the hotel manager. "That you now have found two necklaces?"

Antonio, always the attentive host, nodded. "Your coffee is cold and you have not finished your pastry," he said, his voice seeking to keep her calm. "I can have a fresh order brought to you if you wish."

"Forget the coffee and the damn pastry," Signora Conte said, "and answer my question."

"It's true," Captain Murino said. "Last night there wasn't a single necklace to be found. This morning, we have discovered two. Or I should say, to be accurate, that it was Antonio's staff who found the items."

"But how can there be two?" Signora Conte asked. "When there was only one stolen?"

"I have no answer to that question," Captain Murino said. "I came here to see you, not only to inform you of this development but to see if perhaps you could supply an explanation for us."

"Me?" Signora Conte said. "Why would I know the answer? I don't even know where the necklaces were found. And which of them is mine. For all I know they are both fakes planted by the thief to help clear her name."

"If that were the case, Signora," Antonio said, "she would need to simply replace one necklace, not two."

"As to where they were found," Captain Murino said, "that is one question I can answer. One was in the employee lounge.

That was the first necklace found, and Antonio called as soon as the discovery was made. Now, if that were the only necklace, that would place an even greater suspicion on Loretta, the chambermaid you accused of the theft."

"Well, it certainly doesn't clear her of the theft," Signora Conte said. "In fact, just the opposite. It is proof positive that she is as guilty as I suspected."

"I never said it was found among Loretta's belongings," Captain Murino said. "Since she no longer works here, there are no belongings to speak of. What I did say was that a necklace was found in the employee lounge, and every member of the staff has access to that area. But that, for the moment, is beside the point."

"And what is the point, Captain?"

"Two points, actually," Captain Murino said. "The first is, what are we to make of the second necklace? And then, the answer to the question, which of the two belongs to you?"

Signora Conte sat back and stared at both men. "Where was the second necklace found?" she asked.

"In your room," Antonio said. "In fact, in the exact spot where you told me you had last seen it."

Signora Conte slammed an open hand on the table. "Well, isn't that clever of young Loretta," she said, her voice rising, a mix of anger and frustration. "It's an old cliché, is it not, Captain? That a thief always returns to the scene of the crime."

Captain Murino shrugged. "I've heard it once or twice," he said. "Never witnessed it. I wrote it off as something that occurs only in movies. But if Loretta did indeed return the necklace to where you last claim to have seen it, then why the need for a second necklace?"

"Perhaps to confuse you, as it so clearly has," Signora Conte said. "You may well be dealing with a young lady who is much more sophisticated than she would, at first glance, seem. She returns the actual necklace to its original place and then places a second one in the lounge area, giving the appearance that someone is looking to make her a scapegoat for something she did not do."

"And where do you think a young woman of limited financial means would be able to get such a necklace?" Captain Murino asked.

"That is not a question for me to answer," Signora Conte said.

"I'm curious," Captain Murino said. "You've asked a few questions and made several judgments regarding the two necklaces that have been discovered. Astute judgments, I might add."

"I like to think I'm nobody's fool, Captain," Signora Conte said.

"But there is one question you have not asked," Captain Murino said.

"And what question would that be, Captain?" Signora Conte asked.

"You have yet to ask if you can see either necklace," Captain Murino said. "To see if, indeed, one of them does in fact belong to you. After all, the recovery of a lost family treasure should be, I would think, your main focus. The crime solving, if there is a crime to be solved, should best be left to me."

Signora Conte gave both men a glimmer of a smile. "I was just getting to that very point, Captain," she said. "I'm afraid the sudden appearance of two necklaces caught me off guard and I lost my focus."

"With the captain's permission, I can take you to see both necklaces," Antonio said. "You can examine them at your leisure, and, with luck, one of them will prove to be yours."

"I would be happy to do that," Signora Conte said. "And if one is mine, I'll take it off your hands, pack my belongings, and be on my way. The sooner I am off this island, the happier I will be."

"You can identify the necklace as belonging to you," Captain Murino said. "And nothing would please me more if that turns out to be the case. But I'm afraid I can't let you leave with it."

"Why not?"

"It would be considered evidence," Captain Murino said. "Whether Loretta, or whoever stole it, then returned it does not excuse anyone from having committed a crime. But that's a minor point. There's a much larger matter that has been brought to my attention. And until that matter is resolved, the necklace must remain in police custody."

"Both of the necklaces?" Signora Conte asked. "Or just the one that may be mine?"

"The more valuable of the two," Captain Murino said. "Which, no doubt, will be the one you will claim as your own." He reached into a side pocket of his uniform jacket and pulled out a folded piece of paper. "I received an email early this morning from the carabinieri office in Milan."

"What does that have to do with me or my necklace?" Signora Conte asked.

"When you first reported the theft, I alerted the branches of the carabinieri, from Naples to Lake Como," Captain Murino said. "Gave them a full description of the necklace you reported stolen and asked that they be on alert for any known fences looking to pawn off the expensive piece."

"In the event the thief from Ischia was looking to move it off the island," Antonio added.

"And what response did you get?" Signora Conte asked.

"Until this morning, no such necklace had been found or fenced," Captain Murino said. "But then, last night, in Rome, the carabinieri were called to the home of the Baroness Di Meglio."

"She has been a guest here several times," Antonio said. "A very wealthy woman with a kind heart and a warm soul."

"It seems the Baroness has been traveling," Captain Murino said. "In Switzerland. When she returned, she discovered a valuable piece was missing from her jewelry collection. And she called in the police."

"I'm sorry to hear that," Signora Conte said, sitting up now, both hands gripping the edges of her chair. "But I don't see what her missing jewelry has to do with my leaving Ischia with my necklace."

"I'm afraid, Signora, the piece the Baroness is missing matches the very description of the necklace you accused Loretta of stealing," Captain Murino said.

"So, what?" Signora Conte said. "My necklace is valuable, but it is not the only one of its kind in Italy."

"Most likely that will be the end result," Captain Murino said. "If so, you can be on your way. Until then, the necklace stays under the care of the carabinieri."

"And you, Signora, will continue to enjoy your stay at the hotel," Antonio said.

Signora Conte pushed her chair back and stood, looking down at the two men. "Now I stand accused," she said in a voice loud enough to be heard by the pool area. "I have gone in a span of days from a victim to a thief. In your eyes, I am a suspect, no longer merely an innocent pawn."

Captain Murino eased his chair back and stood facing Signora Conte. "When it comes to matters of crime, I have learned there are very few innocent pawns," he said. "We all have something we wish to keep buried from prying eyes."

The captain turned and walked from the terrace, heading for the hotel exit. "I leave you in Antonio's capable hands," he said as he left. "My men are in the employee lounge and outside your room. You can examine both necklaces at your leisure."

Antonio glanced at Signora Conte and smiled. "Are you sure you would not like a fresh cup of coffee before we begin?" he asked.

34.

THE YOUNG WOMAN walked out of the Cinema Excelsior, gripping tightly onto her daughter's right hand. She looked both to her left and right, the crowd around her dispersing in all directions, and spotted Nonna Maria under the shade of a pine tree, across from the Cinema. She crossed the street and stepped in next to Nonna Maria, her daughter still dutifully by her side.

"Did the little one like the movie?" Nonna Maria asked.

The young woman nodded. "Very much," she said, looking down at her daughter and smiling. "Angela is obsessed with animals, especially horses, so she loved every minute of it."

"My grandchildren are the same way," Nonna Maria said. "And my own children before them. They find comfort in the company of animals, real ones or those they see in movies or on television."

"Inside, before the movie, you mentioned that you know my mother," the young woman said. "Are you a friend, or one of her customers? She has so many of both it is often hard for me to tell one from the other."

Nonna Maria smiled at Angela as she spoke. "Do you have time to take a walk while we talk?" she asked the young woman.

"I'm heading for the port and you and the little one will be looking to head back to Barano. We'll pass the bus stop on our way. It will give us plenty of time."

The young woman hesitated. "What is it you want to talk to me about?" she asked.

"What I have to say will not be easy for you to hear," Nonna Maria said. "Or believe. But you need to trust me, Assunta. Every word is the truth. A truth that has been kept hidden from you for years."

"How do you know my name?" Assunta asked.

"Let's begin our walk," Nonna Maria said, "and I will tell you all you need to know."

They walked slowly, Assunta close to Nonna Maria's side, little Angela closer to the curb, gazing at each store they passed. Assunta looked up at the sky, the dusk bringing with it a string of ominous-looking clouds. "I hope I make it home before the rain comes," she said. "It doesn't rain often in Ischia, but when it does, it feels as if the world is about to end. Thankfully, the showers never last for long."

"My grandnephew Pietro's store is a few meters away," Nonna Maria said. "He will be more than happy to give you an umbrella."

Assunta smiled at Nonna Maria. "Wouldn't he rather sell me one than give it to me as a gift?"

"Pietro's got a good head for business," Nonna Maria said. "He owns a number of shops throughout the island and he won't be thirty until this winter. He has always understood that a gift today guarantees a customer tomorrow."

"You're an interesting woman, Signora," Assunta said. "And,

from what little I've seen, a shrewd one. I have a feeling our meeting at the cinema wasn't quite as accidental as you made it seem."

"It wasn't," Nonna Maria said. "I had been told by a friend that you never miss a chance to take your daughter to the movies and that the first showing is always your preferred time. And please don't call me 'Signora.' It's been years since I've been called that."

"What should I call you?"

"What everyone else does," Nonna Maria said, "friend or enemy. They all call me Nonna Maria."

"Do you have as many friends as you do enemies?" Assunta asked.

"More friends than enemies," Nonna Maria said. "Enemies don't seem to live as long as friends. At least that has been my experience."

"What is it you wish to tell me, Nonna Maria?" Assunta asked.

They were approaching a wooden bench next to a large fountain, shaded on all sides by a thick patch of pine trees. "Let's sit for a while," Nonna Maria said. "The trees will protect us in case the rains come earlier than we expect."

Assunta nodded, and the three walked toward the bench and sat down. "Before I begin, I ask only that the story I am about to tell, you share with no one," Nonna Maria said. "At least for now. Until the truth finally comes out, you must keep what you hear to yourself."

"Why?"

"For your safety," Nonna Maria said. "And that of your child."

Assunta took a deep breath and held Angela closer to her side.

"If you mean to frighten me, Nonna Maria, you have succeeded," Assunta said.

"Be worried, not frightened," Nonna Maria said. "You are a smart young woman and you will know enough to be on your guard. And I will make sure no harm will come to you."

"What is this all about?" Assunta asked.

"It's about a young woman, close to your age, who fell in love with the wrong man and suffered for that mistake," Nonna Maria said. "But some light came out of the darkness. A child, a daughter. But then that too was taken from her; she was prevented from holding her daughter and loving her and caring for her in the way you do all these things for Angela."

"Is this woman someone I know?" Assunta asked.

"She is someone who you should have known but were never allowed to know," Nonna Maria said. "She was not part of your life, and those that knew her, even those she considered friends, led their lives as if she never existed. Mentioned by no one and invisible to all."

"Who is she?"

"Her name was Fernanda Matturana," Nonna Maria said. "At this moment, her name means nothing to you. She is the woman who was found dead in Barano several nights ago."

"I heard about a woman's body being found on the side of the road," Assunta said. "I never heard her name."

"That's because only a few know that name," Nonna Maria said. "But it is a name you should know, and hers is a story you must hear."

"Why?"

Nonna Maria stared at Assunta for a moment, fighting back the urge to shed tears. "Because that woman, Fernanda Matturana, was your mother," Nonna Maria said. "Your real mother."

35.

CAPTAIN MURINO SAT across from Nonna Maria, her large dining room table filled from one end to the other with platters piled high with food, interspersed with bottles of mineral water and carafes of chilled white wine. Captain Murino's carabinieri jacket was resting on the arms of his chair and the sleeves of his starched white shirt were rolled to the elbows. He looked at the table and smiled. "You shouldn't have gone to all this trouble," he said. "I was pleased to receive your invitation to dinner, but was expecting no more than a bowl of pasta with perhaps a salad. What you have here is a feast with enough food to feed a dozen guests."

"I wasn't sure what you liked to eat," Nonna Maria said. "So, I put out a little bit of everything. And what you can't finish, I'll pack for you to take back to the station house to share with the other officers."

"I don't know where to start," Captain Murino said. "Everything looks so delicious."

"I would start with the fish salad," Nonna Maria said. "The fish were caught this morning and have been marinating in oil, lemon, and garlic since I had my first coffee. Then move to the pasta with clams and mussels in a red sauce. After that, rest for a bit while we talk, and then move on to the main course. The broiled branzino, with olive oil, herbs, and a touch of balsamic vinegar. And add to it all the side dishes—the marinated mushrooms, fried peppers with capers and olives, grilled artichokes, and the tomato, red onion, and basil salad."

"Is that what you're having?" Captain Murino asked.

Nonna Maria lifted a carafe and filled two glasses. She slid one to Captain Murino and brought the other to rest next to her right arm. "The food is for you," she said. "The wine is for us to share. And don't forget the bread, it was baked fresh this morning. It can't be called a meal without a loaf of fresh bread."

"Thank you," he said. "Not just for the delicious meal I will soon enjoy, but for asking me to your home. I think the two of us have some catching up to do."

Nonna Maria took a sip of her wine and nodded. "I don't want you to think I have been working behind your back, Captain," she said. "There were reasons for the actions that were taken."

"I trust you, Nonna Maria," Captain Murino said, unfolding a white cloth napkin and placing it on his lap. "I have since we first met six years ago. And, as I've said on more than one occasion, your instincts about people and their actions are better than those of any officer I have encountered in my years as a carabiniere."

"That's because the carabinieri you work with are as young as you are," Nonna Maria said. "They haven't crossed paths with as many people, good and bad, as someone as old as I am."

"With that, let's begin, then, with what should be the simpler of the two cases," Captain Murino said. "Signora Conte and her claims of a stolen necklace."

"She now needs to decide which of the two necklaces belongs to her," Nonna Maria said.

"You never believed she was in possession of a necklace," Captain Murino said.

"I have no reason to change my mind, Captain," she said.

"Do you have any friends in Rome?" he asked.

"I have a friend who has a friend in Rome," Nonna Maria said.

"And how did your friend get his hands on what I've been led to believe is a very valuable necklace?" Captain Murino asked.

"He's an old man now," Nonna Maria said. "Even older than I am. But in his younger days, my friend the Pirate traveled throughout Europe, both for business and pleasure."

"The Pirate is the old man who lives on a motorboat?" Captain Murino asked. "The one who helped us on the last case we worked together?"

"I don't know where he lives," Nonna Maria said. "It's his business where he spends his nights, not mine. What I do know is that many years ago, he was in love with a beautiful young woman from the North."

"A beautiful young woman from Rome would be my guess," Captain Murino said.

"Even though they were in love, they were aware they could never marry," Nonna Maria said. "She was royalty and wealthy. He was neither one. Her family would never have accepted someone from his poor background. They weren't the first couple to be faced with this problem. The distance between

North and South in our country has always been about rich and poor, upper class and lower. It was true then and remains true to this day."

"So, while this young couple never married, they stayed in touch through the years," Captain Murino said. "And one became the famous Pirate of Ischia. And the other?"

"Stayed in the life she was born into," Nonna Maria said. "A baroness at birth and until death."

"So, the necklace in Signora Conte's room belongs to the Baroness," Captain Murino said. "How did it find its way to Ischia?"

"The Baroness spends a month every season in Ischia," Nonna Maria said. "It is nothing more than one friend doing a favor for another."

"And you expect Signora Conte to claim the necklace as her own?" Captain Murino asked.

"I hope she does," Nonna Maria said. "That will not only make her a liar but also a thief."

Captain Murino wiped his mouth and sat back in his chair. He stayed silent for a few moments. "What if she claims the other necklace?" he asked. "The one in the staff lounge."

"She won't," Nonna Maria said. "Signora Conte knows the difference between a necklace of value and one that can be bought at any shop on Via Roma."

"But she can't simply claim the necklace," Captain Murino said. "She will need proof she is the owner."

"If I'm not wrong, Captain, this is not the first time Signora Conte has tried something like this," Nonna Maria said. "It is her way of making a living."

"Which means the insurance company documents she produces as proof of ownership are not authentic," Captain Murino said. "But by looking at whatever she presents to me, I won't be able to tell if they are fraudulent or not. I have limited experience in these matters. Fortunately for us, I know someone who can help."

Nonna Maria smiled. "I'm not the only one with friends willing to help in a time of need," she said. "You seem to have a few friends of your own."

"Not as many as you, Nonna Maria," Captain Murino said. "But I'm doing my best to catch up."

"In time you will," Nonna Maria said. "In any line of work, especially one like yours, the more friends you have, the better off you find yourself."

"It's quite a puzzle we are piecing together, Nonna Maria," Captain Murino said. "And we have yet to get to what is the more crucial of the two cases. The murder of the woman in Barano."

"I have some information to pass on to you about that," Nonna Maria said. "But before we begin, I need to ask one question?"

"What?"

"Do you want Fernet-Branca with your coffee and pastries?" Nonna Maria asked. "Or Sambuca with three coffee beans?"

36.

IT WAS WELL past midnight. Nonna Maria and Captain Murino were leaning against a railing along the Lido, staring out at the lights that flickered and glimmered from neighboring islands and the city of Naples. On a moonlit, cloudless night, they all appeared close enough to touch.

"It is a heart-wrenching story, Nonna Maria," Captain Murino said, "but one as old as the island. Young woman falls in love with the wrong man, bears his child, and is then forced to abandon it, out of fear and shame."

"It happened more during the war years," Nonna Maria said, "when the island was occupied first by Nazis and then by American soldiers. I used to hear my mother and her friends, sitting around the piazza, talking about women who left Ischia never to return."

"The soldiers promised love and devotion and then left soon as their orders came through," Captain Murino said. "It wasn't just here on Ischia that these affairs occurred. I know of several cases in Florence. One involved my mother's cousin. She had a child with a man she fell in love with and they even got to the point where they spoke about marriage."

"But then the truth rose to the surface, like pasta in a pot of boiling water," Nonna Maria said. "He was a married man."

"With a family of his own, and not eager to start a second," Captain Murino said. "But at least in that case, the woman kept her child. Her family moved her farther north and, once there, she made a new life for herself."

"Your mother's cousin is one of the lucky ones," Nonna Maria said. "Fernanda's child was taken from her. Assunta never knew about her real mother."

"And Fernanda never made an attempt to contact her or come back to Ischia to see her?" Captain Murino asked.

"Not until the day she was killed," Nonna Maria said. "After all those years away from her daughter, her family, her home, she came back and was killed here, a few nights ago."

"Do you know if she married or had other children?" Captain Murino asked.

Nonna Maria shook her head. "A few years back, maybe five, six years ago, a friend ran into her at an outdoor market in Salerno," she said. "They had known each other since they were children. She was still a beautiful woman, much like the one in the photo I showed you, but she wasn't the same. She was dressed in black, as if she was in mourning. She had suffered a loss, only her loss was alive and well and living in Ischia."

"One of my officers got a fax from Naples late last night," Captain Murino said. "He had sent a copy of the death certificate to the various field offices and one of them was able to locate the dead woman's dental records. They gave us a name to go with the body."

"The same name I gave you?" Nonna Maria asked.

Captain Murino nodded. "Now that we have a name, we can narrow down our list of suspects," he said. "Starting with her former lover, Carlo."

"He is guilty," Nonna Maria said. "Even if he wasn't the one to bring an end to her life. He is guilty of taking the joy she could have known out of it. It didn't need to end as it did, back then or now. The blame rests at his feet."

"How well do you know him?"

"He was never a friend," Nonna Maria said. "Not to me and not to my husband. On occasion his wife, Gemma, came into our shop to buy groceries. She always brought one of her children along, sometimes the one who resembled Fernanda."

"I don't understand why Fernanda's family turned their back on her," the captain said. "She was their youngest daughter. Carlo is not the only guilty party in this sad affair."

"It was as much out of anger than shame," Nonna Maria said. "People on this island love to talk about what goes on in other families. But when the finger is pointed at them, they grow silent as stone. It's true today and was truer back twenty-some years ago. It was easier to turn their backs than to have neighbors point fingers."

"What will happen now that Fernanda's daughter knows the truth about her real mother?" Captain Murino asked.

"It depends as much on the daughter as it does on the family she was told was her own," Nonna Maria said. "They will tell her not to believe what I told her, and that may be enough. They raised her well and loved her. It can be difficult to turn your back on that and embrace a woman you have never known.

There will be anger and tears, and there will be many questions the family needs to answer."

"That's for them to sort out," Captain Murino said. "But for me, there is only one question I need answered. I know the why, the when, and the how. All that I am missing is the who."

"The simplest puzzles are sometimes the hardest to solve," Nonna Maria said. "At least that's what one of my granddaughters tells me when we sit and try to put together one of her puzzles. This puzzle we face points to an easy answer. And the easy answer is often the wrong answer."

37.

NONNA MARIA SAT facing the pristine expanse of the Spiaggia dei Maronti in the borough of Barano. She was at a small table, her back resting against a brightly painted wooden wall. Gigi's Restaurant was located in the middle of the Spiaggia, a beach that was considered by many travel experts to be one of the most beautiful in Europe. On this sun-drenched morning, tourists and locals had already claimed their place for the day, spreading towels over the white sand and opening chairs under the shade of wide blue umbrellas.

Gigi stood next to her table, staring out at the sparkling waters, a wide smile on his face. "I miss being out on the open water," he said, as much to himself as to Nonna Maria. "This business feeds my family and it has served me well. But the years I spent working on the fishing boats fed my soul. There are moments during the day, especially when every table here is taken, both inside and out, when it is all I can do not to run down those steps, across the hot sand, and jump into that clear water and swim until I can no longer move my arms."

Gigi was in his mid-forties, shirtless, barefoot, and wearing blue and white shorts. He had a thick head of brown hair and a neatly trimmed beard. His once-muscular frame had begun its slow surrender to too much wine and pasta.

"You sound like my sons," Nonna Maria said. "They have a business that only grows bigger by the season. The work is hard, the hours long, much like your job. But it fills their pockets and feeds their families. Yet they talk about how they miss their years on the water and wish they could swim so far out that no eyes could ever see them. It is the dream of every boy who has been raised on this island. Many of the girls, too."

"But not you, Nonna Maria," Gigi said, turning to face her. "If it's true what I've heard, you never go to the beach, despite living so close to so many of them all you need to do is reach out a hand and you can touch the sand."

"I like to stare out at the sand and the sea," Nonna Maria said. "It's like looking at a favorite photo and letting those moments bring back all the memories that photo holds. The water never leaves you, Gigi. It is a part of anyone who calls this island home."

Gigi turned when he saw the woman approach. "This must be who you've been waiting to see," he said.

"She is," Nonna Maria said.

"I hope she's not like you and doesn't eat or drink anywhere but in her own kitchen," Gigi said. "If all my customers were like you, I wouldn't be able to sell a meal."

"But then you would be able to swim all day, instead of just dreaming about it," Nonna Maria said.

"I'll go and put on a pot of coffee," Gigi said, heading inside the restaurant. "And start preparing for the lunch crowd. Leave the two of you to talk in private."

The woman approached Nonna Maria's table, pulled out a chair, and sat down. "It's been a long time since I last saw you," the woman said. "We have both aged quite a bit since then."

She was in her early fifties, thin, her brown hair combed straight back and kept in place by a silver clip. She wore a red beach dress, the bathing suit underneath visible through the transparent fabric. She placed a pack of Lord cigarettes on the table, pulled one out of the pack and held it in her right hand.

"You know why I asked to see you?" Nonna Maria asked.

"There can only be one reason," the woman said, "given that we were never the closest of friends."

"There was a time when we could have been," Nonna Maria said. "But that moment has faded."

"So, you want to talk about the one they found dead on the road," the woman said. "I know as much about her as anyone else on the island. Which is not very much."

"We're both too old to play games, Louisa," Nonna Maria said. "So let's not waste what little time we each have left. The one found dead on the road has a name, and it is one you know well. And your sister and her husband know even better."

"That's you talking," Louisa said. "Not me."

"You were once good friends," Nonna Maria said. "Enjoyed many summer days on the beach and long nights at the Bar Calise."

"I have a lot of friends," Louisa said. "Then and now."

"But she was your best friend, at least for a time," Nonna Maria said. "Until she fell in with Carlo and turned her life upside down. And then you turned your back on her, just like everyone else."

"Including you," Louisa said.

Nonna Maria nodded. "Yes," she said. "I am just as guilty."

"What did you expect me to do?" Louisa asked. "Choose her over my sister? Choose a friend over blood? Not in this world and not on this island."

Nonna Maria leaned closer against the table. "That was true then," she said. "Is it still true now?"

"What are you asking?" Louisa said.

"How did Gemma know the woman was back in Ischia?" Nonna Maria asked. "She had to have been seen by someone. Who better to recognize her than an old friend from the past? A friend who would know her even after all the years that have passed."

"Gemma is my sister," Louisa said. "And she has suffered as well. She made sacrifices few would have made in her place. This other woman means nothing to me. Alive or dead."

"The carabinieri now know her name," Nonna Maria said. "They know it as well as you do. Fernanda Matturana. And I have met her daughter. She finally knows the truth about her mother. Her real mother. And it won't be long before the secret that has been buried all these years is the talk of every piazza in Ischia."

"People are always going to talk, there's nothing to be done to stop the gossip," Louisa said. "On this island, it is practically an occupation for many. But I'm surprised you are a part of that chorus. I've never known you to be one to spread rumors about anyone."

"I don't spread rumors and I don't gossip," Nonna Maria said. "I only listen and believe when I know what I'm hearing is the truth. And we sit here, face-to-face, and both know what will be said about Fernanda is the truth."

"Even if it is, what do you expect me to do about it?" Louisa said. "You can't take back what has been done. Gemma raised the baby as if she were her own. How many wives do you think would have done the same? I don't think I would have been able to do what she did. And I'm not sure you would have been able to, either."

"I wouldn't have to," Nonna Maria said. "I would never take a child away from her mother and call the baby my own. I would not have turned my eyes from my husband's betrayal and let him abandon a woman he claimed to love. I would never live a lie, which is what you and your family have done all these many years."

"We can't all be saints like you," Louisa said. "Some of us have to find solutions to the problems we face. You may not agree with those solutions, but decisions needed to be made, and a family had to be kept together."

"I'm not a saint, Louisa," Nonna Maria said. "But I don't hide from the truth. And the truth is that Fernanda deserved better than to have her baby taken from her, be forced to leave her home and family for decades, and then, when she finally found the courage to return to Ischia, she was killed, tossed out on the street like an old blanket."

"What do you want from me?" Louisa asked. "Will saying I'm sorry make it all go away? Will saying a novena for Fernanda's soul help ease the pain she must have felt all those years? What has been done cannot be undone. It lives in the past and nothing can be changed. No matter how you feel about it or I feel about it."

"I'm not talking about the past, Louisa," Nonna Maria said. "I'm talking about the present. The first wrong done to Fernanda cannot be corrected. But a price for the second wrong must be paid in full. And this time, no one will be able to keep it from being known. This will not be a secret that can be buried with silence. The answer will be known to everyone. And it is an answer I believe you already know."

Louisa glared at Nonna Maria, her clenched hands resting on the wooden table, the unlit cigarette cast aside. The sun warmed half her face, the other was hidden by the shade of an overhead umbrella. "The answer to what question?" she asked.

"Who killed Fernanda Matturana?" Nonna Maria said.

38.

CAPTAIN MURINO STOOD on the terrace of Arianna Conte's second-floor suite at the Grand Hotel Excelsior, gazing down at the thermal-heated swimming pool below. Behind him, Signora Conte was holding the valuable necklace that had been found in her suite. "I don't know how I can ever thank you and your men for finding my necklace," she called out to him.

Captain Murino turned and walked into the large, stylishly decorated room. His footsteps echoed off the blue-marble-tiled floor as he watched Signora Conte gently hold the necklace in both hands. "Are you certain it is the right one?" he asked.

"There is no doubt, Captain," she said. "What I have in my hands is the stolen necklace. The one that never should have been taken from this room in the first place."

"I'm sure you are correct," Captain Murino said. "But it might be wise to, at the very least, take a look at the second necklace."

Signora Conte looked up at him and shook her head. "There is no need, Captain," she said. "The one I have in my hands is the only one I need to see."

"What do you make of the second necklace?" Captain Murino asked. "Does it not seem strange that here we were searching for one necklace only to have two show up on the very same day?"

"There is only one suspect you need to look to for an answer," Signora Conte said.

"Loretta," Captain Murino said. "The one you accused of stealing the necklace that you have in your possession."

"Who else is there, Captain?"

"I can see returning the one she allegedly stole," Captain Murino said. "Once you have it back, there is no longer a reason to charge her with theft. But why a second necklace? Only one is needed to remove the question of guilt. A second necklace opens the door to a number of troubling questions. All of which I'm afraid I'm duty bound to ask."

"What sort of questions?" Signora Conte asked, resting the necklace on top of a glass-topped bureau.

"To whom does the second necklace belong, is the first question that comes to mind," Captain Murino said. "I know you are certain that the one here in your room is yours, but you might, in your excitement of the moment, be mistaken. It could well be the second one is actually yours. And if it is not yours, does that mean there has been a second theft?"

"What would make you think there would be a second theft?" Signora Conte asked. "In the same hotel? By the same accused thief?"

"To this moment, Signora Conte, you are the only one to have labeled Loretta as a thief," Captain Murino said. "We have no other witnesses. No one my men spoke to ever saw her with the necklace or heard her make mention of one. And as far as we can ascertain, she lacks the connections and the ability to move any stolen item, let alone a valuable necklace, into the black market. And now that not one but two necklaces have surfaced, I believe we can safely remove the label of thief from Loretta's name."

"And where does that leave you, Captain?" Signora Conte asked.

"A bit confused, I admit," Captain Murino said. "But I have to believe all will be sorted out in due time. But until then, you will continue to remain here as a guest of the hotel. Whether you will be charged for the room from this point forward I leave up to the discretion of Antonio, the hotel manager."

"Now that I have my necklace back, there is no reason for me to stay on this island," Signora Conte said, her voice loud enough to be heard in the hall behind the partially opened front door. "And you can't make me stay. No crime has been committed. I withdraw any charge I placed against the young woman. She is free and clear."

"It's not as simple as you make it sound," Captain Murino said. "To begin with, I do have the authority to impel you to remain, if not here at the hotel, certainly on the island. And though you assure me that you indeed have your necklace back in your possession, I'm afraid I will need more than your word on the matter."

"Why is my word not enough?"

"You reported the necklace as stolen," Captain Murino said. "A necklace that, up to that moment, no one had seen. Not a guest of the hotel, not a member of the staff, none of the drivers who drove you around the island, nor any of the diners in the restaurants where you had your meals. Not a single soul could identify the necklace."

"So, while Loretta is no longer considered a thief, I'm now considered a thief!" Signora Conte said. "I have to admit, the locals here in Ischia are unlike any I've ever encountered. And I include you in that group, Captain."

"I'm not a local," Captain Murino said. "I'm from Florence. But in my six years working on the island, I've not encountered many serious issues with any of the locals. When problems do appear, they are most often brought in by someone not from Ischia."

"What will it take, then, Captain, for me to take my necklace, pack my clothes, and leave Ischia?" Signora Conte asked.

"Proof that the necklace on that bureau does belong to you," Captain Murino said. "Official proof."

"And how do you plan to get this official proof?"

"I have already started the process," Captain Murino said. "Either later today or first thing tomorrow, an insurance investigator from the company holding your policy will arrive from Naples. They will examine the necklace, and if the investigator confirms that it is indeed the one you have insured, then you will be free to leave."

"How did you know which insurance company I placed my necklace with?" Signora Conte asked, speaking now in a much lower voice.

"There are only six insurance companies in Naples that insure necklaces as valuable as the one you claim belongs to you," Captain Murino said. "I had my men call all six. At the same time, I requested carabinieri offices from south to north to refine their search and do the same. They were given the description, the alleged value of the necklace, and your name. Before the third espresso of the day, the insurance company was found."

"All for a necklace you never believed actually existed," Signora Conte said.

"I admit, Signora, I had my doubts about the necklace," Captain Murino said. "Perhaps I have been a member of the carabinieri for too many years. Even my fiancée accuses me of not believing any story until I have proof of its veracity."

"I pity your fiancée," Signora Conte said.

"But I do believe the necklace is a valuable piece of jewelry," Captain Murino said.

"And what of the second necklace?" Signora Conte asked. "Will the insurance investigator examine that as well?"

"As to its worth and ownership, yes," Captain Murino said. "No one has as yet claimed it. It will be examined, dusted, and photographed, and information will be sent off to all carabinieri offices and to the Rome Art Squad, since it is one of their functions to chart such items."

"For what purpose?" Signora Conte asked.

"To try to find its rightful owner, if such an owner exists," Captain Murino said. "Or to see if it was stolen, and if so, from where and whom. It would be ironic, would it not, Signora, if that second necklace turns out to be the one that leads us to an actual thief."

"Whether that second necklace is stolen or not matters little to me," Signora Conte said. "I have my necklace back. The other necklace is your concern, not mine."

"Then you have no worries, Signora Conte," Captain Murino said. "As soon as the insurance investigator certifies that the necklace is yours, you will be free to leave the island."

"It can't happen soon enough to suit me," Signora Conte said.

"Those are my feelings as well," Captain Murino said.

39.

NONNA MARIA WATCHED the young man tie up the last of the umbrellas and lay a folding chair flat on the warm sand. He looked up at the darkening sky, reached down for his sandals, and headed up the wooden steps, eager to bring an end to his long and hot workday.

When he reached the top step, he turned right and walked toward his black Vespa, parked at an angle and resting against the side of a low cement wall. He was surprised to see Nonna Maria standing next to the Vespa, her black tote bag upright on top of the wall, a folded white handkerchief clutched in her right hand. The young man smiled when he saw her. "Do you need a ride?" he asked.

"Not as long as I can walk," Nonna Maria said, returning the smile. "But I would like a few minutes of your time. If you grant me that favor, then I'll do one for you in return."

"What can you do for me?"

"You work as the bagnino at Michele a Mare's beachfront restaurant," Nonna Maria said. "Have for the last two seasons. The pay is enough to keep some euros in your pockets, but a waiter's salary would put even more and prepare you for what you most want."

"And what would that be?" the bagnino asked.

"To have a restaurant of your own," Nonna Maria said. "Here on the beachfront, where you can feed the tourists and still get a tan."

"And you know all this how?"

"You're young and work hard," Nonna Maria said. "Michele himself told me so."

"You know Michele?" the bagnino asked.

"Since he was a boy," Nonna Maria said. "His father ran this place before him, and Michele worked the same job you're doing. Now he owns two places, one here, the other in Forio. I won't be around to see it, but I expect one day you will be in the same position."

"So, if I give you more time than I already have, what can I expect in return?" the bagnino asked.

"One of Michele's waiters has been offered a job in Naples," Nonna Maria said. "At twice the salary, and more in tips. He leaves next week. I spoke to Michele and asked him to give you the waiter's job once he leaves."

"Why would you do something like that?" the bagnino asked. "For someone you don't even know. And why would Michele agree to it? Just because you asked him?"

"He didn't need much convincing," Nonna Maria said. "As to why I asked him to promote you, it is because I need answers to some questions, and from what I hear, you are the one who has those answers."

"Who did you hear that from?"

"People who have little to do but talk," Nonna Maria said.

The bagnino looked at Nonna Maria for a moment and then nodded. He sat on his Vespa and leaned forward, his arms resting on the handlebars. "Just a few minutes, then," he said. "It's the least I can do for someone who helped me get promoted. My name is Alberto, but you probably already know that."

"I do," Nonna Maria said.

"So, what questions do you want to ask?" Alberto said.

"This past weekend, you were working late," Nonna Maria said. "Saturday night."

"Yes, I was," Alberto said. "Saturday night the tourists tend to linger on the beach longer than they normally do. Which means I don't get to clean up until much later. By the time I'm done, it's after sundown."

"And while you were finishing your work, did you happen to hear a man and a woman arguing on the beach?" Nonna Maria said.

"I heard some locals," Alberto said. "They were shouting in dialect. They were off in the corner, just beyond the bar. But the sound carries by the water, especially when the beach is empty."

"So, you heard every word?"

"Pretty much," Alberto said. "I listened closely because I found myself interested in the argument they were having."

"Argument about what?"

"It was like listening to one of those soap operas my mother likes to watch," Alberto said. "The man was saying how sorry he was for how everything turned out, said he never meant to have it end the way it did. He thought of her every night, every day, all these years."

"And what did the woman say?" Nonna Maria asked.

"That he abandoned her," Alberto said. "Stole her baby and left her."

"Anything else?" Nonna Maria asked.

"He told her he gave her child a better life than she would have had," Alberto said. "He loved the child more than any of his other children. He said his wife never forgave him for being forced to raise someone else's daughter."

"Do you know these two people?" Nonna Maria asked.

"I've seen the man," Alberto said. "He comes to the beach sometimes with his wife and children. His family owns the furniture store about a kilometer from here. My mother shops there when she needs something for the house."

"How did he behave toward the woman?" Nonna Maria asked.

"At first, he sounded as angry as she was," Alberto said. "But then, once she started to cry, he calmed down and tried to comfort her. Told her he would send her money. But she said she didn't want any money, especially not from him."

"Did she say what she did want?"

"To finally meet her daughter," he said. "To be able to tell her she was her real mother."

"How did he respond?" Nonna Maria asked.

"He said his wife would never agree to such a meeting," Alberto said. "He had given her his word when they first brought the baby home that she was never to know her real mother. He told the woman she needed to leave Ischia before anyone recognized her and especially before his wife found out she had returned. He told her he cared about her, but that was something he could never allow to happen. His wife would go mad if it did."

"So, the man had no objection to the woman seeing her daughter and telling her the truth," Nonna Maria said. "It was his wife who wanted the secret kept."

"The woman even asked if he could bring her daughter to Naples to see her," Alberto said. "Without his wife knowing. He told her his wife would somehow find out."

Nonna Maria reached for her black tote bag and then turned to face Alberto. "You will do well in your new job," she said. "Hard work always pays off in the end."

"Have I told you what you needed to know?" Alberto asked.

"All that and more," Nonna Maria said.

"Can I ask you a question now?" Alberto asked.

Nonna Maria rested the black tote on her shoulder and nodded. "Was the young woman the man and lady argued about Assunta?" he asked.

"Do you know her?"

"We were in middle school together," Alberto said. "And she comes to our beach every day with her little girl. They rented an umbrella and two chairs for the season."

"And the little girl's father," Nonna Maria said, "do you ever see him?"

"His name was Domenico," Alberto said. "He was one of my best friends. We were on the Ischia soccer team together."

"Where is he now?" Nonna Maria asked.

"He died in a motorcycle accident down by the port two summers ago," Alberto said. "Domenico had a bad habit of going too fast on his Moto Guzzi 999 and he never wore a helmet. His front wheel hit a stone on the road and the bike flipped over. He landed head-first against an iron pylon where the big boats are docked. He died where he fell, less than two weeks before he was to be married to Assunta."

"I remember hearing about that," Nonna Maria said. "He was the son of one of the tour boat owners."

"He was studying at the academy in Procida," Alberto said. "He wanted to sign up and work on the cargo ships that leave Naples in the winter and return in the spring. The hours and the time away from home are difficult, but the pay is enough to earn a down payment on a house. A house for him, Assunta, and the baby."

"There is a sad cloud following that family," Nonna Maria said. "And the cloud grows bigger and darker by the day."

40.

ARIANNA CONTE SAT in the passenger seat of the red Fiat 500, lighting her first cigarette of the day. Guido Bernardino sat behind the wheel, his window rolled down, his long-sleeved white shirt streaked with sweat spots. It was late morning and the sun was already bearing down on the small car parked in an empty piazza near the Punta Molina Hotel.

"Can we go for a walk while we talk?" Bernardino asked. "It's like sitting in an oven in this car."

"It would be smarter if we didn't," Signora Conte said. "I don't think it's wise for us to be seen together."

"What difference does it make if we're seen walking or sitting in a parked car?" Bernardino asked. "Whoever you think may be watching will still be able to see we're together."

"Just deal with the heat," Signora Conte said. "The sooner you tell me what I need to know, the sooner you can drive away. Then you can get all the fresh air you desire."

"I did as you requested," Bernardino said, resigned to his overheated state. "I found a necklace, and two nights ago I put it in the lounge where the workers change and take their coffee breaks."

"Where did you get the necklace?"

Bernardino turned away from the open window and looked at Signora Conte. "It would be better for both of us if you didn't have that information," he said. "You asked me to get a necklace and I got a necklace."

"How much is it worth?" Signora Conte asked.

"Very little, I would imagine," Bernardino said. "It's a knockoff. There was no sense taking a risk for a piece that would be handed over to the police or, at best, given to you to take home."

"What about the second necklace?" she asked. "How did you manage to get your hands on such an exquisite piece of jewelry in such a short time? A big leap from an inexpensive knockoff."

Bernardino shook his head, a confused expression on his face. "What second necklace?" he asked. "You only asked for one, not two."

"There was a necklace back in my room," Signora Conte said. "Placed in the exact spot where I claimed the one I owned was taken. All it took was one look and I knew it had to be worth several hundred thousand euros. I was hoping to claim it and leave the hotel and the island. But the captain of the carabinieri wouldn't allow it."

"Of course not," Bernardino said. "He needs to verify it belongs to you, and that can only be done by the company where you have your insurance policy. A policy, mind you, for a non-existent piece of jewelry."

"He has an insurance investigator coming to examine the piece later tonight or early tomorrow," Signora Conte said.

"Were you able to give him the name of the company and

our contact there?" Bernardino asked. "He will easily declare you the owner of the necklace and then you can be on your way. He will, no doubt, submit a bill for his services. A substantial bill, I would imagine, given how valuable you claim this second necklace appears to be."

"I didn't have a chance to give him the name of our contact," Signora Conte said. "The carabinieri captain had already lined up an investigator of his own from the same insurance company."

Bernardino looked away from Signora Conte and gazed out the window. The car was parked high enough to offer a scenic view of the Bay of Naples and the white sandy beach below. "That means he didn't believe your story," he said. "That necklace belongs to someone, Arianna, but it's not you. Which puts you in a tight corner when that insurance investigator tells him you have no such necklace insured by their company."

"The carabinieri captain would not have been the one to place the necklace in my room," Signora Conte said. "That would be entrapment, and he doesn't seem the type to play fast and loose with the rules."

"But someone did," Bernardino said. "I doubt it was the cleaning girl you accused of stealing your necklace. She wouldn't know how to get her hands on as valuable a piece as the one placed in your room. It has to be someone with solid connections. I don't know anyone in that hotel who fits that description."

Signora Conte lit another cigarette and tossed the match out her open window. "The old widow," she said as much to herself as to Bernardino.

Bernardino laughed and shook his head. "If that's your only suspect, then you might as well have me drive you to the port, get a ticket for the next hydrofoil, and get you off this island," he said. "Which, by the way, you should do no matter who it was that placed the necklace. This job is not turning out the way you envisioned."

"You want me to pack it in?"

"On this one, yes," Bernardino said. "If you leave now, they have you on little other than reporting a theft of a necklace you never possessed. Once you're off this island, why would the carabinieri captain go crazy hunting you down? He'll consider the case closed and go about his business."

"I'm not one who surrenders easily, Bernardino," Signora Conte said. "You have known me long enough to know that. I will leave this island. But I won't be leaving empty-handed. I'm taking that necklace with me."

"With the carabinieri watching your every move, along with every employee at the hotel?" Bernardino said. "Not to mention the old widow you seem to think is pulling the strings in order to help the girl."

"The necklace is no longer in my room," Signora Conte said. "The carabinieri captain has it."

"That makes it easier, then," Bernardino said. "All you need to do is go to his office and ask for it back. I am sure he will be eager to return it to you."

"He will have to give it to me," Signora Conte said. "If the insurance investigator examines it, checks for its value and pedigree, and determines the necklace is indeed mine."

"The insurance investigator has already been selected by the company," Bernardino said. "Someone you yourself said will be here in a matter of hours."

"An insurance investigator the carabinieri captain has never laid eyes on before," Signora Conte said. "He will check identification and documents, a mere formality, before handing the necklace to the investigator."

"Exactly," Bernardino said. "As soon as that exam is completed, your little game will be revealed and your real problems begin. Right now, they only suspect you were out to shake down the hotel. They can't arrest you on that alone. But the investigator can open up doors that as of now are safely sealed."

"Not if the investigator that arrived was on my side," Signora Conte said. "Someone who would stand to profit from my leaving the island with the necklace wrapped around my neck."

"And where do expect to find such an investigator in such a short span of time?" Bernardino asked. "And a corrupt one, to top it off."

"I know exactly where to find one," Signora Conte said. "And we won't need to worry about a second investigator showing up in the middle of it all. One quick phone call to the right person can solve that minor problem for us."

"You forget, Arianna," Bernardino said, "there is no us. I told you I would get a necklace for you and I did. That is as far as I'm willing to take this adventure of yours."

"What is your fee for finding the necklace and placing it in the employee lounge?" Signora Conte asked.

"For you, the usual," Bernardino said. "Twenty-five thousand euros. Which I would prefer you pay me before I head back to Naples."

"And what if there was an additional one hundred and fifty thousand euros added to your current fee?" Signora Conte asked. "What would that amount get me?"

Guido Bernardino wiped the sweat from his brow with the right sleeve of his shirt and smiled. "It would get you a partner," he said. "And if you rounded the entire fee to two hundred thousand euros, it would also land you a trusted friend."

"Let's not get ahead of ourselves, Bernardino," Signora Conte said. "A partner is all I need. The rest I can handle on my own."

41.

NONNA MARIA STOOD across from the Church of San Giorgio, the parish church of Barano. She gazed up at the tall, slim bell tower, the sun coloring the stucco walls a bright shade of orange. The church, originally built in 1600, was last remodeled in 1773 and has, throughout the centuries, withstood attacks from a varied array of opponents, standing in witness to much civil discord and two world wars. Nonna Maria was one of the few who did not attend church services on a regular basis, and whatever her religious beliefs, she kept them to herself. She never went to confession nor took part in any religious ritual other than funerals and weddings, and even those she avoided if she could.

Yet despite those feelings, Nonna Maria loved living on an island surrounded by churches. She loved the many nights devoted to celebrating the birth of various saints, especially the feasts of Saint Anne and of Saint Giovan Giuseppe, the patron saint of Ischia. Nights that always ended with massive displays of fireworks. She loved to hear the bells ring throughout the day. And she took pleasure in her close friendships with many of the island's clergy, both nuns and priests, some of whom she had known for decades.

Nonna Maria turned away from the tower when she saw the elderly priest wave at her from the entrance to the church. He was short and bald, and not even a thick black robe could hide the girth that had grown considerably in the years since the two had first met. He wore black sandals, and the cap on his head bore the insignia of the Naples soccer team emblazoned in the center. "I always knew it," he said to Nonna Maria from across the way. "Your parish may be at the port in Saint Peter's. But your heart has always been here, in Barano, with Santo Giorgio. And his magnificent tower, built in his honor. He may be the patron saint of the island, but I'm certain Giovan Giuseppe would give up such an honor to have a tower built in his name."

Nonna Maria walked across the street and smiled at the old priest. "It's too late to ask him, Don Bruno," Nonna Maria said. "He's been dead for centuries."

He reached for Nonna Maria and clasped both her hands in his. "It's good to see you, my old friend," he said. "Too long a time has passed. At our ages we can't afford to have many long gaps between visits."

"That's true, and I'll make sure to visit more often," Nonna Maria said. "And you should, on occasion, come down to the port, sit at my table, and have a meal and a few glasses of cold wine."

"Now, I have known you since we were both young enough to run from the port to this church," Don Bruno said. "Which means I know that this visit is not simply a casual one. You need to ask something of me. True or not?"

Nonna Maria nodded. "I gave it quite a bit of thought before I decided to come here," she said. "I need answers to some delicate questions. I will try to ask them in a way that you will be free to answer without betraying your vows."

"It sounds serious," Don Bruno said. "While you enjoy the sun, I will rest here under the shade and do my best to answer your questions."

"My questions have to do with the murder that occurred down the road," Nonna Maria said.

Don Bruno folded his hands and shook his head. "A tragic affair," he said. "I have included the poor soul in my prayers since I first heard of the incident."

"Has anyone come to speak to you about the murder?" Nonna Maria asked.

"If you're asking what I think you're asking, I'm afraid I cannot answer," Don Bruno said. "I cannot repeat to any living soul anything said to me in the privacy of a confessional booth."

"I'm not asking to reveal what anyone told you," Nonna Maria said. "I'm asking you to reveal what wasn't said."

"There are limits even to that, Nonna Maria," Don Bruno said. "I can't reveal identities or discussions. I'm as bound to my word as is any doctor or lawyer. You know that even better than I do."

"What if the person I'm asking about is dead?" Nonna Maria asked. "Are you still bound not to reveal what was said and who said it?"

Don Bruno stayed silent for a few moments. "I usually hear confessions on a Saturday," he said. "I would not be breaking my vows if I told you who I happened to see in church on a particular Saturday. But I cannot tell you what was said between us."

"Even if they spoke to you outside the confessional booth?" Nonna Maria asked.

"If the conversation was of a sensitive nature, it wouldn't matter where it was told to me," Don Bruno said. "Inside a church or out here on the street, it must remain a sealed conversation."

"Do you remember Fernanda Matturana?" Nonna Maria asked.

"Sadly, I do," Don Bruno said. "I was a young priest back then, but even I was aware of the talk surrounding her and Carlo. I don't know the details of how and why she left Ischia, but I was saddened to see her leave."

"She was pregnant with Carlo's child," Nonna Maria said. "Now a young woman with a daughter of her own. It was Fernanda's body found on the road, Don Bruno, left there by her killer. Now, that killer needs to be found. Is our talk here one that you cannot reveal to anyone?"

"Yes," Don Bruno said. "I cannot tell anyone what we have discussed here today."

"Carlo is Assunta's real father," Nonna Maria said. "But Gemma was not her mother. He and Gemma raised Assunta as one of their own. They gave her a good home and treated her with love and affection. But in return, they ruined a life. Fernanda's. They forced her into leaving the island. They forced her to abandon her daughter and live as if the child never existed. I don't know all the sins as well as you do, Don Bruno. But does what was done to Fernanda not count as a grave sin?"

"Yes, it does, Nonna Maria," Don Bruno said. "Just as it is a sin to share a bed with a married man. It is no secret she and

Carlo were having an affair. At the time, it was the talk of Barano."

"But then the years pass," Nonna Maria said. "Gemma returns from Naples with a new baby in her arms. Fernanda no longer lives on the island. People's memories fade, and what was talked about then is forgotten now. Until Fernanda returns. Then what was long ago buried comes back to the surface. And to keep the talk of years ago from starting up again, a life that had been left in shambles needed to end."

"I know what you're thinking, Nonna Maria," Don Bruno said. "And I can help steer you away from those thoughts. I cannot mention a word of what is said between me and someone who comes to confess or confide. But in this case, I believe I can tell you what was not said."

"Tell me," Nonna Maria said. "Help me as much as you can."

"Carlo did not kill Fernanda Matturana," Don Bruno said. "I know he's a prime suspect, as he should be. The carabinieri think he did it, for the many obvious reasons. As I believe do you."

"You are sure he's innocent?" Nonna Maria said.

"I would never venture to call Carlo an innocent man," Don Bruno said. "He has committed his fair share of sins. More than most men. But this murder is not one that can be placed on his hands."

"Do you know where he was the night of the murder?" Nonna Maria asked.

"That I cannot reveal to you," Don Bruno said.

Nonna Maria looked away from Don Bruno and scanned the

empty street outside the church. "Someone must know," she said, as much to herself as to Don Bruno.

"Someone does," Don Bruno said.

Nonna Maria turned back to look at Don Bruno. "Who?"

"You've gotten quite a bit of sun during our talk here today, Nonna Maria," Don Bruno said. "You might have gotten too much. Your arms may well burn a bit later tonight. You might want to arrange a visit from your nephew the doctor and see him about getting some cream before the pain settles in. The sooner the better."

42.

GEMMA LEANED AGAINST the iron railing of the terrace, gazing down at the passersby. She and her family lived in a large house in Barano, but she and her husband also owned a two-bedroom apartment in a three-story building in Ischia Ponte. They would often stay there after a night spent in the port area rather than make the thirty-minute drive back to their home.

Carlo came out onto the terrace, rested a bottle of red wine on the center of the glass-topped table, and stared at his wife. "It's only a matter of time, Gemma," he said, his voice filled with anger, his words slurred from the wine he had been drinking. "They will figure out what happened. If not the carabinieri captain, then Nonna Maria for sure."

"I'm not the only guilty one in this, Carlo," Gemma said. "Fernanda's death is on you as much as it is on me."

"You didn't have to do what you did," Carlo said. "We could have found another way."

"I was not going to let that woman take my daughter away from me," Gemma said. "Or my granddaughter. I love them both too much to have allowed that to happen."

"She didn't want to take them away," Carlo said. "All Fernanda wanted to do was to meet them, get to know them, spend some time with them. She had a right to do that. It was us that took that away from her."

"Us?" Gemma said. "There is no us in this. It was you, Carlo. You were the one that got her pregnant, and you were the one who talked me into bringing her child into my home."

"It was wrong of me to do that, I know," Carlo said. "And I have paid a painful price for it all these years."

"What price, Carlo, have you paid?" Gemma asked. "Back then you chased any woman that caught your eye. You ignored me, the wife who loved you, to spend your nights in the arms of women whose names you barely knew. Men like you don't pay any price. You leave the suffering to others."

Carlo poured himself a large glass of wine and drank half of it in one swallow. "It was wrong of me to behave the way I did," he said. "I admit that. But none of those women took me away from you. It was your bed I returned to each night. I always came back."

"That may have been true with all the others," Gemma said. "But not with Fernanda. You were in love with her, and if you were a real man, if you could stand on your own two feet instead of living off your family's money, you would have left me for her. That you cannot deny."

"I wish Louisa had never told you Fernanda was in Ischia," Carlo said. "I would have taken care of the situation on my own. And if I had done it my way, we wouldn't be in this mess."

"I didn't need Louisa to tell me anything," Gemma said. "I saw Fernanda with my own eyes, that morning she arrived."

Carlo rested his glass on the table and walked closer to Gemma. "Where did you see her?"

"At the pier," Gemma said. "I drove down with Assunta and Angela to buy some fresh fish for dinner. I was bartering with one of the fishermen when I turned to look around me and there she stood, staring at Assunta and the child."

"You recognized her?" Carlo asked. "After all these years?"

"How could I not?" Gemma said. "Every time I look at Assunta, I see Fernanda's face. It was her, and all it took was that one look and I knew what I needed to do."

"She must have followed you home," Carlo said. "That's how she knew where we lived."

"We're not that hard to find, Carlo," Gemma said. "I saw her a second time when I went into the garden to get some fruit for dessert. And that's when she saw me."

"You should never have confronted her," Carlo said. "She might have been content just to see Assunta and the child. Maybe that's all she wanted."

"I didn't mean to do her harm," Gemma said. "I waited a few hours, debating whether to meet with her or not. Then I stepped into the alley off the garden and motioned for her to come over. She hesitated at first, then slowly made her way to me. It was dark by then and just the two of us standing there, not speaking, not knowing what to say, not even after all the years that had passed."

"And then what?"

"I asked her why she had come back," Gemma said. "What it was she wanted."

"And?" Carlo asked.

"She wasn't here just to look at Assunta and her daughter," Gemma said. "She was here to take them both from me."

"Did she say that?"

"She didn't have to," Gemma said. "It was in her eyes, in the way she moved and the way she looked at me. She was a mother returning to claim her child."

"You could have turned your back on her, Gemma," Carlo said. "We could have explained it all to Assunta. She would have understood. You're the only mother she has known. The only mother she has loved. She would never leave your side, especially for the woman who abandoned her as an infant."

"I couldn't take that chance," Gemma said, speaking now as if in a trance. "My mind went blank. All I felt was rage. I thought we had her out of our lives. But there she was, standing before me, defiant, determined. There was only one way for it to end. I reached for her, wrapped my hands around her throat, using a strength I didn't even know I had. I kept them there even as she sank to her knees, her hands gripping my arms. I kept them there, even after I knew she was gone."

Carlo walked over to Gemma and stood next to her. "We need to get away, Gemma," he said in a soft voice. "Get off this island. And we need to do it soon. No one but me knows what you did. No one else knows how it happened. They might suspect us. But they lack proof. They'll keep digging, no doubt. But there were no witnesses to what you did."

Gemma turned to face Carlo and slowly shook her head. "Wrong again," she said. "There was a witness that night. Someone who saw everything. Someone who could put us both in prison for the rest of our lives."

43.

GUIDO BERNARDINO SAT across from Captain Murino, watching as he scanned the thick batch of papers handed to him moments earlier. Bernardino was dressed in a cream-colored jacket, white slacks, a blue shirt, and a shiny pair of penny loafers. He sat straight up in a straw-backed chair and wiped his upper lip and brow with a folded white handkerchief. He stared at the carabinieri captain, who had not yet bothered to make eye contact with him. Finally, the captain rested the papers on his desk and smiled up at Bernardino. "I'm pleased to see the insurance company chose to send someone as experienced in these matters as you seem to be."

"This is a delicate matter," Bernardino said. "And it requires someone who can distinguish an expensive piece of jewelry from one that can be purchased at any open-air market. Given the nature of the complaint, the company thought it best to send their most experienced investigator."

"I'm glad to see they took the matter as seriously as they have," Captain Murino said.

"As they should," Bernardino said. "Especially given the fact that a young woman's guilt or innocence hangs by the decision."

"Where did you get that particular piece of information?" Captain Murino asked. "There wasn't any mention of a young woman in my report to the company. I merely asked them to send an investigator to prove the necklace in question does indeed belong to Signora Conte and that it is in fact insured by your company."

Bernardino took a moment to compose himself before answering the question. "I heard talk," he said. "Some fellow workers at the company mentioned that Signora Conte had called and reported a theft. And then I was later informed that, in fact, the necklace she believed a maid had stolen had been found back in her room."

"Did Signora Conte contact you directly?" Captain Murino asked. "At any point since this situation first presented itself?"

"No," Bernardino said. "There would be no reason for either of us to have any contact. She has someone at the company who handles her affairs. I'm merely an investigator brought in to determine the authenticity of the item in question."

Captain Murino sat back in his leather chair and folded his hands across his chest. "Have you ever been to Ischia?" he asked. "Prior to today, I mean."

"My first time," Bernardino said, attempting to appear relaxed but troubled by the carabinieri captain's questions. "It seems a beautiful island. But, sadly, I won't be here long enough to do any sightseeing. Once I authenticate the necklace, I must return to the home office."

"How long have you been doing this type of work?"

"About six years," Bernardino said. "I was an appraiser prior to that and then was fortunate to be hired by the company."

"And how many investigators does the insurance company employ?" Captain Murino asked.

"In Naples alone, at least a dozen, if not more," Bernardino said. "Some stay for a few months and move on to a bigger company or a different line of work. Others, like myself, enjoy the work and tend to stay put. As you no doubt are aware, finding a job such as this in Naples with a company in good standing is not easy."

"No, I would imagine it's not," Captain Murino said. "But Rossana has a good instinct as to who to hire and who to shy away from. She always has. Don't you think so?"

Bernardino's mouth was dry and his blue shirt was now blotched with sweat. He shook his head and shrugged. "I'm afraid I don't know anyone named Rossana, Captain," he said.

"You're joking, of course," Captain Murino said, smiling. "Rossana hires all the investigators for the insurance company that employs you. She has for years. And she is the one who decides who is sent out on the various assignments. So, tell me, what is she like to work with? I imagine she can be quite demanding."

Bernardino shook his head, beads of sweat dripping onto his jacket. "I'm not one to gossip, Captain," he said. "With all due respect, I did not come here to discuss the goings-on at the insurance office."

"Yes," Captain Murino said. "You're here to determine the pedigree of the necklace Signora Conte claims is hers. And to assure me that it is indeed a necklace insured by the company that employs you. Those are the only reasons you are here, in Ischia, sitting across from me."

"That's correct, Captain," Bernardino said.

"And here I am rambling on with questions about your qualifications and trying to elicit some bits of gossip about Rossana," Captain Murino said. "I seem to be wasting your time as well as mine. And for that I apologize."

"No offense taken, Captain," Bernardino said, feeling as if he were back on solid footing. "You were merely curious, which, I expect, is one of the many factors that make you good at your job. But now I think we should get on to the matter at hand. Signora Conte's necklace."

"It looks as if you've already reached your conclusion," Captain Murino said. "Calling it her necklace. This despite the fact you have yet to lay eyes on it."

"Merely a figure of speech, Captain," Bernardino said. "Nothing more to it than that, I assure you."

"Before we get to the necklace, permit me two more questions?" Captain Murino said.

"Are they absolutely necessary?" Bernardino asked.

Captain Murino leaned forward in his chair, both elbows on his desk, a harsher tone to his voice. "I'm afraid I must insist," he said.

"Very well," Bernardino said. "Ask away, then."

Captain Murino opened the top drawer of his desk and pulled out a thick yellow folder. He placed it on his desk and opened the flap. "I spoke to Rossana last night," he said. "Truth is, she and I have been in contact since Signora Conte first reported the alleged theft. I took the accusation seriously, despite my doubts. She did some digging of her own and discovered that Signora Conte had no such necklace insured by her company. The very same company you claim to work for as an insurance investigator."

"But that's impossible," Bernardino said. "If she were not insured, then why would I have been sent here to examine the necklace?"

"Perhaps it's because you are no more an insurance investigator than I am an astronaut," Captain Murino said. "Now, you can be detained on any number of charges, some of which can put you away for quite a number of years. Not only by my office here in Ischia—those charges are minor and would get you only a few months in prison at most. But with Rossana's aid, I expanded my search. It seems you have played this game many times in the past. And you were successful at it. Rossana tells me your insurance investigator ruse has worked in a few other cities—Turin, Genoa, and Positano, to name just three. Working off her description, I wired the carabinieri offices in those cities, and, no surprise, each one is prepared to charge you with offenses much more serious than the ones you face here in Ischia. You have accumulated quite a track record for yourself. But one thing you've said to me today seems to be true."

"And what would that be?" Bernardino asked, sitting now relaxed, free to no longer pretend to be someone other than himself.

"You do know your jewelry," Captain Murino said. "As a fence and as a thief. I have no doubt you acquired enough knowledge down the years to be an excellent insurance investigator."

"And all along, I thought it would be the old woman who would cause me the most grief," Bernardino said.

"You were right to be worried about Nonna Maria," Captain Murino said. "I have never met anyone who has lived in one place her entire life and yet has the contacts of someone who has traveled the world."

"How did she connect me to you?"

"Through Rossana," Captain Murino said. "She is Nonna Maria's niece, and she helped guide me through the complicated waters of the insurance industry and bring you to my attention. So, yes, Nonna Maria had a hand in putting you in your current situation."

"So, what happens now?" Bernardino asked.

"That is what I'm going to leave for you to decide," Captain Murino said. "I can hold you here or have two of my men escort you to one of the cities eager to charge you and leave your fate in their capable hands."

"I would like to avoid that scenario if possible," Bernardino said.

"I'm happy to hear you feel that way," Captain Murino said. "And not only am I in a position to help you avoid such a situation, I can also see to it that a few of the charges you currently face can be greatly reduced. Assuming, that is, that you do as I ask."

"What is it you want me to do?" Bernardino asked.

Captain Murino gently closed the yellow folder on his desk and glared up at Bernardino. "I need you to tell me everything you know about Signora Arianna Conte."

44.

THE SMALL MOTORBOAT zigzagged its way through the crowded waterway and under the causeway bridge, making for the dock of Eden, the restaurant with one of the best views in Ischia. The tanned young man manning the motorboat, who had made this journey hundreds of times across three summer seasons, gazed down at the well-dressed woman sitting on the wooden plank. She was dressed as befitted a woman of her age and station, in a short-sleeved blue dress and cream-colored shoes, a hand-knit white sweater braced across her shoulders. Her hair was the color of sand and her clear blue eyes glimmered under the shadows of the fading sun and the spray of the water.

The young man made a sharp right turn, tilting the boat slightly, and rounded a bend, the dock leading to the steps of the restaurant less than fifty feet away. Nonna Maria and the Pirate were standing on the dock waiting. As the boat moved closer to the dock, the Pirate leaned down and eased the boat inches from the landing.

"I've never seen you without your boat," the young man said to the Pirate. "And I've never seen you in anything but a bathing suit. I almost didn't recognize you."

The woman looked up at the Pirate, smiled, and turned to the young man and handed him a fifty-euro bill. "Thank you for the ride," she said, and then stood and reached for the Pirate's outstretched hand.

The Pirate and the woman warmly embraced, and then she turned to Nonna Maria. "It's been much too long," she said to her. "Even though we haven't seen each other for years, you are never far from my thoughts."

"Good friends are never forgotten," Nonna Maria said. "No matter how much time passes between visits. And you have always been a good friend to me."

"And to me as well," the Pirate said, a wide smile on his face, a tight red bandanna stretched across his forehead, his thick, sun-drenched hair tied in a knot and held in place by a red band.

The woman placed a hand on the Pirate's bearded face and looked at the white shirt, sleeves rolled to the elbows, and cream-colored shorts he was wearing. "I've only known you to wear a bathing suit," she said. "Don't tell me you've allowed old age to mellow your rebellious spirit."

"Not a bit, Baroness," the Pirate said. "The shirt belongs to one of Nonna Maria's many relatives. And the pants were loaned to me by a friend in the port. I would not be allowed in the restaurant wearing only a bathing suit. Normally, I would have gone in anyway. But, out of respect for you, I decided it best not to cause a scene."

They walked up the stone stairway, Nonna Maria in the lead, the Baroness and the Pirate close behind. The owner was there to greet them at the top of the stairs. He reached for Nonna Maria's hand and smiled when she stood next to him. "I've been told by many you never eat a meal anywhere other than in your own kitchen," he said to her. "I consider it an honor that you have chosen my restaurant as the first place other than that wonderful kitchen to enjoy a meal. You won't be disappointed, I promise you."

"You have a great kitchen, everyone says so," Nonna Maria said. "But I'm not here to eat, Piero. Or to drink, while we're at it. But my two friends will enjoy your wonderful food and wine. I'll sit with them for a few minutes. We have some catching up to do, and with the view you have, I couldn't think of a better place."

"I have a table in the corner," Piero said, leading the way. "On a clear night such as this one, you can see as far as the lights of Naples."

The water of the bay splashed against the stone walls of the restaurant. It was a large outdoor space, situated between Michelangelo's villa and a thermal spa. The young owner had taken advantage of the vista and, in a few short years, had turned his restaurant into one of Ischia's finest. The table looked past the castle and out toward the open waters of the bay, the lights of the islands of Capri and Procida sparkling in the distance. It was a cloudless night and the sky was as warm and embracing as a soft blanket.

Nonna Maria sat with her back to the water, allowing the Pirate and the Baroness to enjoy the view. Piero approached the table. "Shall we start with some mineral water and a bottle of D'Ambra's finest white?" he asked.

Nonna Maria shook her head. "Not tonight, Piero," she said. "Our friend is from Salerno, which means a bottle of Marisa

Cuomo white to start. And, for an appetizer, bring the mussels you cook over the grill. There are none better on the island."

"You say that without having ever tasted one," he said. "How do you know they are as good as you say?"

"People talk, Piero," Nonna Maria said. "And sometimes they talk about your delicious mussels."

They sat in silence, enjoying the view, and waited until the wine was brought to the table and two glasses were filled before they spoke. "Has the matter with the necklace been resolved?" the Baroness asked.

"Not yet," Nonna Maria said. "But you have helped bring us much closer to solving the puzzle."

"This Signora Conte is now claiming your necklace as her own," the Pirate said, "and is looking to leave the island with it packed in her bags."

"The captain of the carabinieri is keeping her here," Nonna Maria said. "And the necklace is locked safely in his office."

"And your goddaughter?" the Baroness asked. "Has her name been cleared of the theft?"

"It seems that way," Nonna Maria said. "Especially now that there is more than one necklace to be claimed."

"More than one?" the Baroness asked. "How did that come about?"

"It seems Signora Conte tried to pull a fast one and put some secondhand necklace in Loretta's dressing area," the Pirate said. "Make it look like the young girl had really stolen it and was hiding it."

"So, this Signora Conte doesn't work alone," the Baroness said. "She has a partner. The one who planted the necklace."

"But not a loyal one," Nonna Maria said. "He is working with the carabinieri, helping them to paint a full picture of Signora Conte."

"And Nonna Maria pulled the welcome mat from under her feet by having Antonio at the Excelsior put your necklace in the signora's room," the Pirate said. "That, I would bet my sword, was not something she was expecting."

"I have come across many women like Signora Conte in my life," the Baroness said. "They are always looking to take advantage of those without the means to fight back. There are enough innocent victims in this world. We don't need another."

A teenage waiter approached the table and placed a large wooden bowl filled with a steaming pile of grilled mussels in the center. He handed the Baroness and the Pirate each a folded and warmed wet cloth, bowed, and turned from the table.

"I have never had them grilled," the Baroness said.

"Then you are in for a treat," Nonna Maria said. "Piero makes them Ischia style, grilled over a bed of coals, sprinkling them with white wine and rubbing herbs and spices over them as they cook."

"And you have my heart for ordering the Marisa Cuomo wine," the Baroness said. "Each sip I take reminds me of my younger years back in Salerno."

"A good wine brings good memories," Nonna Maria said. "I had my first taste of D'Ambra wine in the shadows of that castle behind me. My husband brought a bottle and two glasses the night he asked me to marry him."

"You were lucky to have had him in your life," the Baroness said. "He was a good man and loved you very much."

Nonna Maria nodded and pointed to the Pirate. "And this good man still carries the torch for his first love," she said to the Baroness.

"Your husband was a good man, Nonna Maria," the Pirate said. "I'm afraid I wasn't as good. But I was crafty enough to survive in the life I chose to make for myself. It was a life that brought me a living, but not without some loss. The Baroness the biggest loss of all."

The Baroness turned to the Pirate and raised her wineglass to his. "I never think of what we had as a loss. The days I spent in your company were some of the happiest of my life."

Nonna Maria smiled and began to ease out of her seat. "Since you seem so pleased with the appetizer, I'll ask Piero to grill you his fresh catch of the day, cooked over an open flame, covered in basil, herbs, lemons, and white wine," she said. "And along with it, a fresh green salad from his garden."

"We'll take our dessert back at the port," the Pirate said. "I asked Gennaro earlier today to slice up some fresh peaches and put them in a carafe of white wine and chill it. We'll have that along with some pastries from Minicucci. He remembered the Baroness had a sweet tooth for his baba and is preparing a batch as we speak."

"The young man in the motorboat will take me back to the port and then return and take you back when you are done," Nonna Maria said.

"Thank you for this special night," the Baroness said, standing to give Nonna Maria a warm embrace.

"And thank you for trusting us with your necklace," Nonna Maria said. "Though I have a feeling that if Signora Conte did manage somehow to make it off the island with it in her luggage, the Pirate would not rest until he found it and returned it to you."

"Is there anything else I can do to help?" the Baroness asked. "I'll be here as long as you need me."

"Where are you staying?" Nonna Maria said.

"She'll be with me," the Pirate said. "And when she's not, she'll be at the Regina Isabella."

"Then there is something more you can do," Nonna Maria said.

"Just say the word," the Baroness said.

"Help us catch a thief," Nonna Maria said.

The Pirate slapped the table and laughed. "Just like old times," he said. "If Signora Conte thought she had her hands full with you, Nonna Maria, wait until the Baroness gets to work on her. She has no idea what kind of storm is heading her way."

Nonna Maria left the Pirate and the Baroness to finish their dinner, walking toward the front of the restaurant, finding Piero waiting by the top of the steps. "Were the Pirate and his guest pleased with everything so far?" he asked.

"You outdid yourself," Nonna Maria said, reaching her hand into her black tote bag. "And your food and wine may have been just the spark needed to relight a romance that went dark many years ago."

"I'm happy to hear that, Nonna Maria," he said. "If you are reaching into that bag of yours for money to pay for the meal, I would be even happier if you stopped right now."

"You run a business, Piero," Nonna Maria said. "And like

everyone else on this island, you have only the summer season to earn enough for a full year."

"I would not have this business if your son hadn't made me see what this island could become and has become," Piero said. "When he first mentioned opening a restaurant, there were but a handful of tourists on the island. I was working at another place, one in Lacco Ameno, and wasn't earning enough back then to pay for cigarettes, let alone rent. But he believed in this island and he believed in me. And it is because of him I own such a beautiful place today. Take a look around. Every table is full, and it is like this every night. Treating your friends to a meal is the least I can do to thank him."

Nonna Maria pressed a hand to Piero's face and smiled. "You have worked very hard for your success," she said. "And I will tell my son about the kindness you have shown me and my friends. But if I were you, I wouldn't mention the free meal to the Pirate. He hears that, and you will be sending over four more bottles of Marisa Cuomo wine to his table."

Nonna Maria then made her way slowly down the sandy stone steps to the motorboat waiting at the dock to take her back to the port.

45.

AGOSTINO STOOD IN the center of Nonna Maria's dining room, his medical bag still held in his right hand. "You, of all people, should know better than to ask me about another patient," he said to her. "Any information between us is private."

"Agostino, I would never ask you to tell me anything you can't talk about," Nonna Maria said. "All I want to know is whether Gemma is a patient of yours and when was the last time you saw her."

"Has this anything to do with the murdered woman whose body was found in Barano?" Agostino asked.

"It has everything to do with it," Nonna Maria said.

Agostino walked closer to the dining room table, rested his medical bag in one corner, pulled out a chair, and sat down. "I never thought I would hear myself saying this," he said, "but I would love a cup of your coffee."

"The way I drink it?" she asked.

Agostino looked at Nonna Maria and nodded. "You only live once," he said. "Let's give it a try."

A few minutes later, they were sitting across from each other, each with a cup of espresso in hand. "I don't know how you can drink one of these, let alone fourteen cups a day," Agostino said. "I've never tasted a coffee this strong. It's making my heart race."

"I never told you I drank fourteen cups a day," Nonna Maria said. "And you should know better than to listen to talk from those who have nothing better to do than talk."

"This is talk I believe," Agostino said. "I normally have your coffee plain, without sugar, and even then it's got a kick to it. What did you add to it?"

"A small piece of dark chocolate, three sugars, and a drop or two of Stock 84," Nonna Maria said. "Without the brandy it would taste too sweet."

Agostino took a last sip of the coffee, rested the cup on the table. "Tell me what you need to know about Gemma and I'll try to answer your questions without revealing any medical information."

"Has she come to see you, or have you visited her, in the last week or so?" Nonna Maria asked.

"I went to see her a few days ago," Agostino said. "Carlo called my practice and asked if I had time to see Gemma when I made house calls in his area. I told him I would, and I did."

"And why did she need to see you?" Nonna Maria asked.

Agostino hesitated before answering. "She had taken a fall," he said. "Tripped over a loose stone on the street near their home. It was late at night, and with the poor lighting in the area, she didn't see the stone in her path. She had a bruised and swollen ankle."

"And Carlo?"

"I was not there to check on Carlo," Agostino said. "Gemma

was the only patient. And since all she had was a minor contusion caused by a fall, I don't feel I betrayed any relevant medical information. By now, all of Barano has been made aware of her injury."

"Did you visit her the day after the body in the road was found?" Nonna Maria asked.

Agostino opened his medical bag, took out a thick black notepad, flipped it open, and scanned the pages. "The next afternoon," he said. "In fact, I went from Gemma's home to the crime scene to confer with the medical examiner, at her request. She called while I was tending to Gemma and asked if I would stop by on my way back to the port."

"Were Carlo and Gemma aware of the woman's body found on the road?" Nonna Maria asked.

"If they were, they didn't mention it to me," Agostino said. "I was only made aware of it when I got the phone call from the medical examiner."

"Thank you for answering my questions, Agostino," Nonna Maria said. "Are you ready for a second cup of coffee and some fresh pastries?"

"My heart has yet to recover from the first one," Agostino said. "And I must pass on the pastry. My wife is preparing my favorite lunch and I don't wish to spoil my appetite."

"In that case, I'll pack them up and you can take them with you," Nonna Maria said. "For you both to enjoy after your meal."

Nonna Maria pushed her chair back, stood, and walked into her kitchen, and came out holding a large plastic bag filled with small boxes of assorted pastries. She handed the bag to her nephew.

"Don't you want to save any for yourself?" he asked.

"I don't like sweets," Nonna Maria said. "Except for the chocolate I put in my coffee."

"Finally, one bad habit I don't need you to break," Agostino said. "By the way, why are you so interested in Gemma?"

"She and Carlo knew the woman found dead in the road," Nonna Maria said. "Back when you were away at medical school and then doing whatever it was you did at that hospital in the North while you were learning to be a doctor."

"My residency," Agostino said.

"And the woman they found was a friend of mine," Nonna Maria said. "It was a story I thought would end in sadness. But I was wrong. It ended in tragedy."

"And you think Gemma and Carlo had something to do with the death of the woman in the road?" Agostino asked.

"They were both there at the start of the story," Nonna Maria said. "And I believe they were both there when it ended."

"The papers you asked me to find, the hospital records," Agostino said. "The dead woman is the mother of the child born in Naples."

Nonna Maria nodded. "And Carlo is the father," she said. "Together, he and Gemma raised Fernanda's daughter, Assunta, as if she were one of their own. And none of it could have been done without the doctor who signed the birth certificate and the Mother Superior who ran the children's ward knowing about it. Fernanda's death touches their hands now, as well."

"And you think Gemma and Carlo had something to do with her murder?" Agostino asked.

Nonna Maria reached over and kissed her nephew on his right cheek. "We must each keep our secrets, Agostino," she said. "You, because of the rules of your profession. Me, because it's my nature to keep silent until I know for certain that what I believe is actually what happened."

"Would it help any if I asked you to be careful?" Agostino asked. "If what you believe is actually true, then there's no telling how they might act if confronted and cornered."

"It would help a little," Nonna Maria said, turning to walk back to her kitchen. "But another cup of coffee would help me even more."

46.

ROSSANA D'ANNUNZIO STOOD on the terrace outside Signora Conte's room. She was in her early thirties, tall, with long brown hair, strands streaked blond by the summer sun, an unlit Lord cigarette held in her right hand. She was dressed in a pale green summer dress, sleeveless, and shiny black pumps. A thin black briefcase rested against the railing of the terrace.

Captain Murino sat on a cushioned lounge chair, the morning sun warming his face, his legs crossed, his hands folded and resting on his lap. They both turned when Signora Conte walked out to the terrace, the necklace curled in the palms of her hands, a wide smile on her face. "You have no idea how happy you've made me," she said to Rossana. "I thought it was lost to me forever. Now it's back where it belongs."

Rossana picked up the briefcase and rested it on the table. "There are just a few formalities still to be completed," she said. "I promise you, it won't take up much of your time."

"What sort of formalities?" Signora Conte asked. "Have I not been through enough already? To have the necklace taken from my room and not know its whereabouts? To have no one believe me when I pointed out the young woman who stole it in the first place?"

The door to the suite opened and Captain Murino nodded to the two young carabinieri standing in the hall. "They can both come in," he said to them.

The Baroness walked into the room first, followed by Nonna Maria. Signora Conte turned and watched them enter. She looked at Rossana and Captain Murino. "What are they doing in my room?" she asked.

"I invited them," Rossana said.

"For what purpose?" Signora Conte asked.

"I can answer that, if you wish," the Baroness said, stepping onto the large terrace. "I'm here to take back my necklace. It has served its purpose. As Rossana and the good captain will both admit."

"Your necklace?" Signora Conte said. "How dare you walk in here and claim my necklace as your own? Is everyone on this island either a thief or a liar?"

"No," Nonna Maria said. "Not everyone."

Signora Conte glared at Nonna Maria. "The old woman," she said.

"I am an old woman," Nonna Maria said. "There are many as old as I am on the island. The tourists believe the thermal baths are why many of us live long lives. I think it's the wine."

Rossana snapped open the black briefcase and pulled out a thick pile of stapled documents. She handed them to Captain Murino. "These documents, Signora Conte, will show that the necklace you are so gently holding in your hands does not belong to you, but is in fact the property of the Baroness. And has been for the many years she has had it insured by my company."

"There's another set of documents here as well," Captain Murino said. "They show that you, through an associate employed by the company, filled out a number of forms that insured various pieces of jewelry that you in truth never owned. You reported a number of them stolen over the years, collected on the policies—again, I emphasize, fraudulent policies—and, in addition, collected money from a number of high-end hotels throughout Italy."

"Those items were properly insured," Signora Conte said, losing a bit of her composure. "And the hotels did pay me money in return for my not mentioning that I had been a victim of a theft while I was their guest."

"The policies were written by someone at the company," Rossana said. "That part is true. His name is Franco Calderieri, and the two of you have been working together for five years, at least with my company. We have been investigating Signor Calderieri for the past few months. This necklace was the final proof needed to end his run. He is now in the hands of the authorities in Naples and has agreed to testify against you. In return, his lawyer has requested a more lenient sentence."

"He was less than thrilled to have learned that while you gave him a cut of the insurance proceeds you collected, you failed to mention the money you received from the various hotels," Captain Murino said. "He feels a bit slighted. And, in my experience, a slighted partner makes for an excellent witness."

"And then, of course, there's your good friend Bernardino," Rossana said. "He will map out the entire scheme for the magistrate, in order to avoid having to spend what remains of his life in an uncomfortable prison cell."

Captain Murino stepped up next to Signora Conte, took the necklace from her hands, and placed it in Rossana's briefcase. "I'm afraid we will need your necklace for a while longer, Baroness," he said. "As evidence at trial. I assure you it will be kept under lock and key and returned safely."

The Baroness looked at Nonna Maria and smiled. "You can keep it for as long as you need," she said to Captain Murino. "But I should tell you, it only looks expensive. It's merely a higher-quality fake than the one Signora Conte's partner placed in the staff lounge."

"So, it's worthless," Captain Murino said.

"Financially, yes," the Baroness said. "But nonetheless it means a great deal to me. It was given to me as a gift decades ago by a dear friend. I wasn't yet a baroness, but he was always a pirate."

"It was a gift from the heart," Nonna Maria said. "That's always worth more than money."

Captain Murino signaled to his two men by the door. "Signora Conte, my men will escort you to the station house," he said to her. "I will try to make your stay with us as comfortable as possible. You won't be with us very long."

"It's now a matter of jurisdiction," Rossana said, taking the documents from Captain Murino and placing them back in her briefcase. "A number of cities have made claims on you. But in this case, I think Naples stands on firm ground as the first city in which you will stand trial."

"I see no need for cuffs," Captain Murino said to his men as they stood on either side of Signora Conte.

As she was led out of the suite, Signora Conte turned and glared at Nonna Maria. "One day, old woman, I will once again be free," she said. "Then I will come back to this island and look for you."

"That meeting will be about twenty years from now, Signora Conte," Rossana said. "If not more."

"In that case, I'll save you some time and tell you where you will be able to find me," Nonna Maria said. "In the cemetery. Buried next to my husband. I'll be waiting for you there."

47.

LORETTA SAW NONNA Maria walk toward the tailor's shop on Via Roma. She crossed the street, dodging a couple on a blue Vespa, and caught up to her just as she was reaching for the door. "I stopped by your house hoping to find you there," Loretta said. "Your tenant told me you were on your way here."

"He's not my tenant," Nonna Maria said. "Il Presidente is my friend."

"Antonio called me at home earlier," Loretta said. "He also had the florist send over a dozen roses, with a note attached."

"What did the note say?" Nonna Maria asked.

"He apologized for letting me go," Loretta said. "And then when we were on the phone he told me I can go back to work starting Monday. But he doesn't want me to be a member of the cleaning crew anymore."

"He's moving you to the waitstaff," Nonna Maria said. "You will be serving drinks and appetizers to the guests on the terrace in the evening. The salary is better, and the tips should match what the guests were leaving in return for cleaning their rooms."

"You have no idea how happy this makes me, Nonna Maria,"

Loretta said. "And none of it would have happened if it weren't for you. I'm sorry I caused you to go to so much trouble."

"It wasn't you that caused anyone trouble, little one," Nonna Maria said. "It was Signora Conte. But now that's all in the past. She will no longer cause you any problems."

"Will they send her to prison?" Loretta asked.

"She will be sent where she deserves to be sent," Nonna Maria said. "But where she goes is not my concern."

"I just wanted to find you and thank you," Loretta said. "I don't know how all this would have turned out if you weren't there to help."

"If you really want to thank me, I need you to do me a favor," Nonna Maria said.

"Anything, Nonna Maria," Loretta said.

"Come into the tailor shop with me," Nonna Maria said. "I'm picking up some clothes he made for my grandchildren and I want him to measure you for a dress I would like him to make for you."

"Nonna Maria, you don't need to have a dress made for me," Loretta said. "You have done more than enough. I thank you with all my heart. But it would be too generous a gift for me to accept."

"Antonio just promoted you," Nonna Maria said. "That calls for a gift. Plus, your birthday is less than a month away. What kind of godmother would I be if I didn't get my goddaughter a gift she deserves?"

"But a dress is too much," Loretta said. "I don't need to wear one for work. We wear the hotel uniform when we're serving the guests."

"The dress isn't for you to wear at work," Nonna Maria said. "It's for when that young busboy, Gaspare, who smiles whenever he sees you, gets up the nerve to ask you out."

"How do you know him?" Loretta asked, blushing. "And I'm not the only girl he smiles at. He smiles at all of them."

"I know his parents," Nonna Maria said. "And yes, he does smile at all the girls. But he has eyes for you and wants to ask you out. Only he's afraid you will turn him down."

"How do you know?" Loretta asked.

"That part doesn't matter," Nonna Maria said. "What does matter is that when he does get up the nerve to ask you and you say yes, that you have a nice dress to wear for wherever it is he will be taking you."

"Why does Gaspare think I'll turn him down?" Loretta asked. "I always make time to talk to him during our breaks. He doesn't say much, so I was never sure if he liked me or not."

"He does, very much," Nonna Maria said. "Gaspare is shy, always has been, even as a little boy. That's a good thing to be, sometimes. My husband was shy, and it took him a while before he asked me out. It's just nerves, nothing more."

"Where did your husband take you on your first date?" Loretta asked.

"For a walk and a gelato," Nonna Maria said. "Down by the Lido. Just the two of us. As we were walking, we passed a small piazza where a man with a guitar was singing an old Neapolitan song. My husband took me in his arms and we danced to that song for what seemed the longest time."

"Did you know on that walk and during that dance that he was the one for you?"

"Yes," Nonna Maria said. "But I had an idea long before then. I had seen him working in the fields with his father. He looked at me and I looked at him. Off that one look, I pretty much knew. I had to wait a few weeks before he got up the nerve to ask my father if he could ask me out. But if it is meant to be, then the wait is more than worth it."

Nonna Maria opened the door to the tailor's shop and stepped inside, holding Loretta's hand. "Now, let's have Peppino get started on making you a beautiful dress," she said. "He's been making clothes for my family since he was your age. And much like a good wine, he only gets better with time."

48.

NONNA MARIA AND Il Presidente walked slowly along the waterfront, glancing at the variety of boats moored in the large harbor. Tourist boats nestled next to custom-made luxury yachts, designed for the wealthy who often made Ischia their prime summer destination. Farther down were the Coast Guard boats, followed in their wake by long lines of small, privately owned boats, many owned by the locals, who would take family and friends out to open waters to enjoy a sun-filled day free of the crowds.

"That first boat on the right," Il Presidente said, pointing to a row of pleasure boats rocking from the lapping waves. "That one belongs to Carlo. He's owned it for as long as I can remember."

"He worked with you for a few years," Nonna Maria said. "Or so I was told."

Il Presidente nodded. "Not so much with me, but for me," he said. "I used him from time to time to move goods from Naples to the island. Black-market cigarettes, whiskey, on occasion clothes. Jobs that I didn't have time to do myself. I was busy with other matters in those days."

"Were you friends?" Nonna Maria asked.

"We weren't close, no," Il Presidente said. "Back then, people like Carlo were willing to work for me because I paid well. But they kept their distance. They were as afraid of me as everybody else."

"So, he wasn't a violent man," Nonna Maria said.

"I didn't need any help on that end," Il Presidente said. "Carlo was just looking to make extra money for his family and for all the women he was chasing. He was not someone to be feared. Unless you were a married man and he had eyes for your wife."

"Then you don't think Carlo is capable of killing someone," Nonna Maria said.

"I think everyone is capable of killing someone," Il Presidente said. "But, in general, I doubt Carlo, unless pushed to the extreme, would bring physical harm to a person. He was not a rough-and-tumble man. He fancied himself more a lover than anything else."

"But when you warned him to stay away from Fernanda, Carlo didn't listen," Nonna Maria said. "He was well aware of your reputation, yet he did not run from it. Not when it came to her."

Il Presidente shook his head. "I will never know how you manage to discover all this information," he said. "It is true, I did warn him to stay away from Fernanda. He had, as you know, many women back then. More than enough to satisfy any man. And Fernanda was an innocent, falling in love with a man who was wrong for her in every way possible."

"Were you in love with her?" Nonna Maria asked.

Il Presidente walked quietly for several moments, the water lapping against the sides of the pier the only sound between them. "A man in my profession couldn't afford to fall in love, Nonna Maria," he said. "Most of my nights ended in spilled blood."

"So, you were looking to protect her," Nonna Maria said.

"And I failed," Il Presidente said. "I threatened him a few times and even beat him on one occasion. But it didn't matter. You can beat a lot of things out of a man, Nonna Maria. But you can't beat out love."

"Then why did he allow her to leave as she did?" Nonna Maria asked. "And why did he hand her baby over to Gemma to raise as their own? And why did she agree to it?"

"None of that had anything to do with love," Il Presidente said. "That was all about money. Maybe Carlo was in love with Fernanda. Maybe to him she was different from all the other women he spent time with. But even so, he could not give up the life his family money allowed him to live. With men like Carlo, love always takes a back seat to money."

"And there was more than enough to pay off a doctor for his silence and a Mother Superior for her cooperation," Nonna Maria said. "And even some to give to Fernanda to help her start a new life and to her mother here in Ischia to keep her lips sealed."

"Those were difficult years for many people in Ischia, as you well know," Il Presidente said. "The tourists had started to arrive, but not in the numbers we see today. A pocketful of money can make even the most honest among us look the other way."

"Carlo kept his money and his easy life and turned his back

on Fernanda," Nonna Maria said. "That leaves Gemma. Why would she take in another woman's child and raise it as her own? It would have been easier for her to turn her back on her husband and the baby."

"No one would have blamed her if she had," Il Presidente said. "Carlo had been cheating on her since their engagement. It was the worst-kept secret on the island. He had no job to speak of, no steady income. His entire existence was dependent on his family's open wallet. Maybe she was a fool as well. Maybe she was as much in love with Carlo as poor Fernanda was. And a fool in love will do most anything to hold on to that love."

Nonna Maria turned to look up at Il Presidente. "Maybe even kill," she said.

49.

GEMMA WALKED WITH the aid of a cane out of the pharmacy in Barano, a short distance from the small church of Saint Rocco. She held a small plastic bag in her right hand, navigating her way around parked cars and a cluster of tourists listening to a guide describe the area and its history in German.

Nonna Maria stepped out of the shadow of Saint Rocco and walked up next to Gemma, startling the younger woman. "Surprised to see you going to church," she said to Nonna Maria. "Especially one outside your parish."

"I wasn't in church," Nonna Maria said. "Just standing in the shade of one."

Gemma continued on her way, her eyes moving from the pavement to Nonna Maria. "There's plenty of shade in the port area," she said. "You don't need to come to Barano to find a cool spot."

"I came to Barano to see you," Nonna Maria said.

"Why do you need to see me?" Gemma asked, her manner gruff.

"I heard you took a fall," Nonna Maria said. "Wanted to

see how you were feeling and if there was anything you might need."

"I don't need anything from you," Gemma said, "other than to be left alone."

"You fell the same night as Fernanda's body was found," Nonna Maria said.

Gemma stopped and turned to face Nonna Maria. "What difference does it make what night I fell?" she said. "And you can't be sure the woman found in the road was Fernanda."

"The carabinieri think it is," Nonna Maria said. "So do I. And, if anyone knows for sure, my guess is it would be you."

"Me?" Gemma asked. "Why me? This Fernanda woman means nothing to me. I'm sorry she died and was found the way she was, but other than that I have nothing to say."

"You know more about her than you admit," Nonna Maria said. "You and Carlo are like many on this island. You keep your secrets sealed and have long ago tossed away the key."

"Rumors," Gemma said, "not secrets. I know there was talk years ago about my Carlo and this Fernanda. But talk is all it was. And as you know better than anyone, talk is the currency of those born on Ischia."

"Most of the time, the talk is not worth a listen," Nonna Maria said. "But once in a while, the words spread have the weight of truth behind them."

"And what truth do you see behind the words spread about this woman and my husband?" Gemma asked.

"Fernanda was in love with your husband," Nonna Maria said. "And the child you came back with from Naples was theirs, not yours. You raised her as your own and loved her. But Assunta is not your daughter. She was Fernanda's child. That is the truth. And we both know it to be so."

"Assunta is my daughter," Gemma said. "I raised her from birth. She was fed and bathed with my hands. The clothes she wore as a child and even today as a young woman with a child of her own, were made by me. Don't you dare say she's not my daughter."

"She knows, Gemma," Nonna Maria said. "Assunta knows the truth. You and Carlo and your friends and family kept it hidden from her. Had Fernanda not returned to see her daughter in the flesh, to meet her grandchild, then it might have been kept hidden until we were all buried under the ground. But Fernanda did come back, and she paid a horrible price for that attempt to see with her own eyes her flesh and blood."

Gemma glared at Nonna Maria, the weight of her body digging into the cane helping to hold her in place. "Were you the one who spoke to Assunta?"

"Yes," Nonna Maria said. "She has a right to know. And she deserved better than to have heard it after her mother was killed and left on the side of a road."

"So, she knows," Gemma said, the anger slowly draining from her voice. "Thanks to you, she knows. You've done what you set out to do. You can go on your way now. Your task is complete."

"Not just yet," Nonna Maria said. "There's still unfinished business."

"What more is there for you to do?" Gemma asked. "You've turned my daughter against me. I'll do my best to heal that wound, but the damage is already done. Carlo will be forced to defend himself against his daughter's many questions. And we will be looked at with hatred by those who once were cherished friends. So, with all that, what else is there for you to do?"

Nonna Maria stared at Gemma and stayed silent for a moment. "To see that the one who killed my friend Fernanda is arrested for murder," she said.

50.

THE STREGA SAT facing the window, ignoring the sheer white curtains brushing against the sides of her face. Her room looked out on a small piazza, the road curved and narrowed around a thick stone planter. Nonna Maria stood next to the Strega, her eyes on the street below, quiet now in the early afternoon hours. "Inside the darkness of this room, people pay you to look into your bowl of water and oil and tell them what their future holds," she said. "But from this window, you don't need a bowl of water and oil to see. All you need are eyes."

"People come to hear what I have to tell them," the Strega said. "No one asks what I have seen."

"I'm asking," Nonna Maria said. "From this window you see all that goes on in the piazza, day or night. You stay hidden from view, no one looks up to your window. Everyone in Ischia has been told from the time they can walk not to stare at a strega. It's part of the power you hold over them."

"A power you don't believe I have," the Strega said. "We are not that much different, the two of us. We both hear and see but only speak when we need to speak. I do what I do for money. You do it to help a friend."

"Enough people believe to keep coming through your door," Nonna Maria said. "I don't need to hear about my future from anyone. I know what waits down the road."

"What is it you think I saw from this window that matters to you?" the Strega asked.

"You were sitting here the night Fernanda Matturana's body was thrown against the wall in the piazza," Nonna Maria said. "You saw who placed it there."

"It was late at night," the Strega said. "The streets are unlit. It would be hard to see anything in the dark."

"Her body was driven to that spot," Nonna Maria said. "The car lights would have been on. It is all you would need to make out faces and figures."

The Strega turned away from the window, took a silk handkerchief from a side pocket of her housedress and wiped at her eyes. "I knew harm would come to that woman the minute she returned to the island," she said. "I felt a strong presence of evil in our midst. I wished so much to warn her, prayed to the heavens she'd come see me, heed my warnings and leave Ischia."

"You knew her story," Nonna Maria said. "Why she had returned. To see her daughter. And her granddaughter. You also knew there would be others who would not allow that to happen. Could not allow it to happen. And would do anything to stop it. Even murder."

The Strega turned back to look at Nonna Maria and shook her head. "I was wrong," she said. "I knew they would not risk having her meet with her daughter. But I chose to ignore the dark clouds I saw in the woman's future and thought a way could be found to get her off the island before such a meeting could occur. A way that would not lead to her death. I wanted to help, but I couldn't. Outside of this room, no one listens to my words. In here, I am a strega. On the street below, I am nothing more than an old woman."

"You can still be a help," Nonna Maria said. "Not as a strega. But as a witness. You saw who tossed Fernanda's body against that wall. You keep many secrets to yourself. But this is one that cannot stay buried. You must bring it out into the light."

"I will never stand before a judge," the Strega said. "It would end me. No one would come see me, pay me to tell them what roads lie ahead. I would no longer be trusted as a strega. I can't allow that to be taken from me. It is all I have in my life."

"No one will know who told me," Nonna Maria said. "Not the carabinieri. Not any magistrate. No one will need to stand in a court and point a finger at anyone who brought harm to Fernanda. They will point the finger at themselves and admit to their guilt."

"How can you be so certain of that?" the Strega asked.

"You have your powers," Nonna Maria said, "and I have mine. Now, please, come closer to the window and tell me what you saw that night."

The Strega hesitated a moment and then eased her chair near the lip of the windowsill. She looked up at Nonna Maria. "I am trusting you," she said. "What I tell you must remain a sealed secret between the two of us."

Nonna Maria nodded. "Till death," she said.

51.

FEDERICO CASTAGNA PARKED his car several meters from the entrance to Gemma and Carlo's home. It was early morning, the sun just beginning to rise above the horizon. Nonna Maria sat across from him in the passenger seat, the black tote bag resting on her lap. "It was kind of you to give me a ride," she said to him.

"After all you've done for me, it's the least I can do," Federico said. "Besides, it's not good for you to be walking to Barano in this heat, even this early in the day. I'm glad I saw you when I did."

"I'll need to speak to them alone," Nonna Maria said.

"I will wait for you," Federico said, "and take you back to the port once you're done."

Nonna Maria looked at Federico and smiled. "You drive well," she said to him. "You should never doubt your abilities."

"More luck than skill," Federico said.

Nonna Maria lifted the tote bag from her lap and reached for the door handle when she saw the blue Fiat pull out of a side street. Carlo was behind the wheel, Gemma sitting next to him. Several pieces of luggage were tied down on the top rack of the car.

Nonna Maria moved her hand away from the door handle. "They're on the move," she said. "And with all that luggage, they're looking to leave the island. Let's put your luck and skill to use, Federico."

Federico started his Fiat 500, shifted the car into gear, and eased into the road. "At this hour there aren't many cars on the road," he said. "They'll know they're being followed."

"Don't let them get too far ahead," Nonna Maria said.

Carlo picked up speed as soon as he cleared out of the piazza. Federico followed at a distance. "He's going well beyond the speed limit," Federico said. "I'm not sure I can keep up. I'm not very good around these curves."

"I trust you with my life, Federico," Nonna Maria said.

Federico shifted into higher gear and was soon right behind Carlo's car. His wheels squealed as he rounded each sharp curve, and sweat started to line his forehead and upper lip. "I don't want to worry you, Nonna Maria," he said. "But my glasses are starting to fog up."

"I'm not worried, Federico," Nonna Maria said.

Carlo's car dodged a fruit cart and hit two cardboard boxes resting near a corner, scattering the cartons and flowers inside against the tables of an outdoor café. Federico's car brushed the side of the fruit cart and sent it tumbling to its side. Behind them, fruit littered the empty road.

"I'm sorry, Nonna Maria," Federico said. "I've never driven this fast before."

"After the next turn, the road goes downhill," Nonna Maria said. "You'll need to go even faster."

"I was praying you wouldn't say that," Federico said.

52.

ASSUNTA SAT ACROSS from Captain Murino. They were in an outdoor café, staring out at the boats in the harbor, two cups of espresso between them. "I'm glad you came to see me," he said. "And I'm sorry for everything that's happened."

"I could have stopped it," Assunta said. "But I froze. I stood there looking down at them both. The woman who had raised me and the woman who was my real mother, glaring at each other. It happened so quickly. One minute they were talking, the next, one was on the ground, dead."

"Don't blame yourself," Captain Murino said. "You have done nothing wrong."

"My life has been a lie," Assunta said. "My history, the family I thought I had, none of it is true. My real mother is dead. And the woman I thought was my mother is the one who killed her."

"It will take time," Captain Murino said. "But you will make your own way. Make your own life. With your daughter by your side."

Assunta nodded and wiped tears from her eyes. "What will happen to Gemma now?" she asked. "And to Carlo?"

"They will both be arrested," Captain Murino said. "One charged with murder, the other as an accessory after the fact."

"It didn't have to end this way," Assunta said. "I could have gotten to know my mother. And I would not have turned my back on Gemma. She loved and cared for me more than anyone ever had."

"I'm afraid life doesn't afford us many happy endings," Captain Murino said.

"I would like to be there, when you come for them," Assunta said. "They will be afraid and I might be a comfort to them."

"You can ride with me," Captain Murino said. "We'll finish our coffee and head to Barano."

"You won't find them in Barano, Captain," Assunta said. "They're leaving Ischia. This morning. On the first ferry."

53.

CARLO'S CAR ZOOMED past two slower vehicles and rounded the turn that led down to the port and the waiting ferry to Naples. Federico, his face now a mask of sweat, jumped the curb and rode on the side grass. He was heading straight for Carlo's car.

"Brace yourself, Nonna Maria," he said.

The two cars collided, sending Carlo's into a tailspin, stopping against a rusty iron pylon. The front end of Federico's car was damaged and lines of white smoke filled the morning air.

Federico's chest had slammed against the steering wheel, causing him to gasp for breath. Nonna Maria scraped her knees against the glove compartment and had a gash on her right hand from slamming it against the broken passenger window.

A cluster of workers circled the cars and eased the four passengers out.

Gemma leaned against her damaged car and watched as Nonna Maria was helped out of Federico's mashed Fiat. She inched past her car and the workers heading back to their jobs and limped toward Nonna Maria.

"You have haunted me enough, old woman," she said, once she got close enough for Nonna Maria to hear. "It's as easy for me to bury two as it is to bury one."

Gemma lunged for Nonna Maria and tossed her to the ground. She looked around and spotted a length of rope on the pier. She bent over and reached for it, folded it in her hands, got to her knees, and stared down at Nonna Maria.

"You have interfered in my life for the last time," Gemma said. "It will be much easier for me to spend the rest of my life in prison knowing I was the one who put you in the ground."

"My mother used to tell me we all will die sometime," Nonna Maria said. "And we all will die somewhere."

Gemma leaned closer to Nonna Maria, the rope wrapped around her hands. Nonna Maria reached out her left hand, grasped Gemma's damaged ankle, and squeezed it with all the strength she had. Gemma reared back, an anguished look on her face, dropped the rope, and fell to the ground.

Nonna Maria struggled to her feet, grabbed her black tote bag, and swung it against Gemma several times, forcing her to cover her face and head. Nonna Maria stood over her now, thin lines of blood oozing down her knees and the fingers of her right hand. "It's over, Gemma," Nonna Maria said. "There's no one left for you to harm."

Carlo came running from around his car toward Nonna Maria. The two stood and stared at each other for a moment. Carlo approached Nonna Maria, gazing briefly down at Gemma. "I know you have no reason to do anything for me," he said. "But still I would like to ask a favor."

"What is it?" Nonna Maria asked.

"Keep an eye on Assunta for us," Carlo said. "Despite all that has happened, we still love her very much."

Nonna Maria nodded. "As if she were one of my own," she said.

54.

CAPTAIN MURINO AND Nonna Maria stood at the pier, watching as Gemma and Carlo were placed in the rear seat of a carabinieri patrol car. Nonna Maria was being attended to by a young EMS technician, who cleaned and bandaged her hand and knees.

"You sure she doesn't need stitches?" Captain Murino asked.

"The cuts are superficial," the EMS technician said. "I didn't find any glass in the open wound on her hand. Antibiotic cream and warm water soaks ought to do the trick. I'll leave her the cream and fresh bandages. She should be healed in a few days."

Captain Murino nodded his thanks and watched as the EMS technician returned to his truck. "You could have been killed," he said to Nonna Maria. "Either in that car or at Gemma's hands. None of this needed to happen. All you had to do was call me."

"I went to Barano to talk to them," Nonna Maria said. "Nothing more than that. And I would have called you if I could. But I don't have a phone."

Federico walked toward them. "The accident was my fault," he said. "If you're looking to blame anyone, Captain, blame me."

"Don't listen to him," Nonna Maria said. "Federico saved

the day. He drives like he was born behind a steering wheel. If he weren't such a great accountant, he would make an excellent carabiniere."

"I'll keep that in mind," Captain Murino said.

Nonna Maria stared at the clump of bystanders that had formed, blocked from the scene by yellow police tape the carabinieri had strung around the perimeter. Nonna Maria knew all of the faces and most of the names of the ones glaring at Carlo and Gemma. "They're angry now," she said. "Yet they kept silent for many years. Each one could have stepped forward and told the truth. There are no innocents here. Not even me."

"There are many reasons why people keep silent, Nonna Maria," Captain Murino said. "Often, it is with good intentions. In this case, for the benefit of the child and to keep Gemma and Carlo's family intact."

"It was easier to believe what they were told than what they saw with their own eyes," Nonna Maria said. "The baby was well cared for, and Gemma and Carlo raised her with love and affection. Fernanda was nowhere to be seen and soon forgotten."

"Now they will embrace Assunta and her child," Captain Murino said. "And Gemma and Carlo's actions will be a story told for years to come."

"In Ischia, we want to believe marriage is meant to last until death," Nonna Maria said. "No matter how many times couples argue or stray or lie, the public face must be that of the happy man and wife. Many things have changed on the island since Fernanda was forced to abandon her baby, but the hold marriage has on us remains strong."

"Not every man is like Carlo, Nonna Maria," Captain Murino said. "You, for example, were married to a man you loved and who loved you in return. What the two of you had is what we strive for, that once the flame of love is lit, it can never be extinguished."

Captain Murino and Nonna Maria turned and walked from the port area. "I never thought of you as a romantic, Captain," Nonna Maria said. "You may have been born and raised in the North, but the years spent on Ischia have warmed your heart."

Captain Murino smiled and glanced at Nonna Maria. "Do you have to be from the South in order to be a romantic?" he asked.

"Yes," Nonna Maria said. "In the South we have cold hands but warm hearts. In the North, it's the other way around. Warm hands and a cold heart."

"If you ever decided to venture off the island, you should take a trip and spend time in Florence," Captain Murino said. "It is an amazing city. The birthplace of Michelangelo."

"He may have been born in your city, but his heart was here, in Ischia," Nonna Maria said. "He built a home not far from here and designed it in such a way that he could see the Castello from each window. That's where the woman he loved, Vittoria Colonna, lived. He would stare out the window every day and not move until he saw her face."

"All the books I've read about him say he was gay," Captain Murino said.

"Of course he was gay," Nonna Maria said. "Why wouldn't he be? He had a beautiful house in Ischia and a woman he loved living on the other side of the water."

"Michelangelo lived to be a very old man," Captain Murino said. "Despite his complaints about his many ailments."

"What was wrong with him?"

"Stomach problems mostly," Captain Murino said. "The diet back then was cured beef, cheese, and bread. It wasn't until the fifteenth century that Florence saw oranges or lemons. His limited diet caused him digestive issues."

"Then he should have stayed in the home he had here," Nonna Maria said. "Even then, we served many of the meals that are served today. He would have his fresh fish each day, a nice tomato and red onion salad with basil and hot cherry peppers, a cold bottle of wine. After his meal, a cup or two of coffee and a nice glass of Fernet-Branca. That would have cured any digestive issues he had."

"Sounds like the perfect cure," Captain Murino said. "Though even the great Michelangelo would have considered your coffee a bit too strong for his taste."

"Not if the woman he loved, Vittoria Colonna, had prepared it for him," Nonna Maria said. "When you're in love, even the bitterest coffee tastes sweet."

Captain Murino glanced at Nonna Maria. "If all the women in the world were like you, we would be living in a much better, saner place," the captain said.

"If all the women in the world were like me, Captain," Nonna Maria said, "they would all be old."

55.

A CROWD GATHERED in a circle around the freshly dug grave of Fernanda Matturana. Nonna Maria stood in the center of the crowd, surrounded by family and friends. They had come to pay their respects to a friend they had, for many years, believed was lost to them.

Pepe the Painter stood on one side of Nonna Maria and Il Presidente on the other. Behind Nonna Maria, along with her children, were Giovanni the taxi driver; Loretta, her goddaughter; Federico Castagna and his sister, Isabella; Rafael the butcher; the Pirate; Antonio from the Excelsior; Don Bruno; and Enrico the jeweler. Captain Murino was on the other side, his back to the calm waters of the bay, standing next to Fernanda's daughter, Assunta, and her granddaughter, Angela.

Pepe the Painter glanced down at Fernanda's coffin, his eyes glistening with tears. "It is a beautiful thing you are doing, Nonna Maria," he said, his voice choked. "To have her buried here, in our beautiful cemetery, among the members of your family."

"She was my friend," Nonna Maria said, glancing up at the marble walls and catching a glimpse of the photo of her husband, Gabriel, placed in the center of his final resting place. "She deserved better than to be left in an unmarked grave."

"We were all her friends," Pepe the Painter said. "And each of us, in our own way, let her down, turned our backs when she needed us."

"We need to learn to live with our mistake," Nonna Maria said. "And do all we can not to have it happen again."

Don Bruno stepped up next to the coffin and offered some soulful words of prayer. Most of those in attendance bowed their head and prayed along in silence. Nonna Maria kept her eyes on the coffin, her memory racing back years, trying to remember when and why she had given up on helping her troubled friend.

Il Presidente rested a hand on Nonna Maria's arm and squeezed it gently. "She didn't want to be found," he said. "If she had, she knew one of us would have come for her. It is a choice she made for herself."

"But not a choice that gave her joy," Nonna Maria said. "Otherwise, she would never have felt the need to return. To see her daughter. She was up against more than she could handle. Gemma had money to spread around and buy silence. Carlo was too weak a man to protest or protect. And the rest of us went on with our lives. She was alone, ashamed, and probably scared. That is why she didn't want to be found. She didn't want to be judged."

"Her friends wouldn't have judged her," Il Presidente said.

"Not everyone on this island was her friend," Nonna Maria said. "There are many here who thrive on pointing out the mistakes of others, happy to laugh and sneer when a back is turned. No one knows that better than you."

Il Presidente nodded. "There are people like that everywhere you go, Nonna Maria," he said. "No matter how beautiful the island or how poor the city. There will always be those who take pleasure in the misery of others."

A crew of four men stood on either side of the coffin, lifted it with a sturdy rope slung under the bottom, and gently lowered it into the open grave. They then reached behind them for buckets full of rocks and filled the hole. The entire procedure took less than fifteen minutes. The crowd watched in silence.

A wooden cross with Fernanda's name was placed at one corner of the grave and a thick bouquet of flowers rested in the center.

Assunta found her way to Nonna Maria and reached down and embraced her and held her tight for several moments. "I can never thank you for what you did for her," she said. "For my mother."

"The grave is temporary," Nonna Maria said. "As you know, our custom is that she will stay in the ground for two years. Then her remains will be dug up, placed in an urn, and put up in the wall, with a photo affixed to the outside of the marble."

"Do you have a place selected?" Assunta asked.

"She will be placed next to the slot reserved for me," Nonna Maria said. "Up there on the left. One day, I'll be with her and with my husband."

"I'll come and visit often," Assunta said. "She spent so many years alone. It will be nice for her to have company for a change."

"She would love that," Nonna Maria said. "Even in death we should not abandon or forget the ones who have left us. I come here twice a week. The caretaker keeps a chair for me. I sit for a few hours and spend time with my husband. Talk to him sometimes. Other times, just sit and enjoy his company. Those are the happiest hours of my week. And the saddest."

"It is a beautiful and peaceful place," Assunta said. "I'm glad my mother is back at home, where she belongs. Where she always belonged."

"That is the best we can hope for from life and from death, little one," Nonna Maria said. "To find the one place where we belong."

56.

CARLO SAT ON a wooden bench, his arms resting between the iron bars of the holding cell. Nonna Maria stood on the other side of the bars, the black tote bag held in her left hand. "I didn't think you would come," Carlo said.

"Captain Murino told me you had something you needed me to do," Nonna Maria said.

"I do," Carlo said. "The manager of the Banco di Napoli is holding an envelope with your name on it. You can pick it up anytime."

"What's in it?"

"Money for Assunta," Carlo said. "Twenty thousand euros. It's all I managed to put away after all these years. A sad sum, I realize. I know it won't undo the hurt I caused her, but I wanted to leave her something."

"Money is always good to have, Carlo," Nonna Maria said. "A mother would have been better."

"She had a mother," Carlo said. "Gemma raised her as if she were one of her own. Everyone knows that, including you."

"It's not the same," Nonna Maria said. "Maybe if Assunta had known the truth from an early age, had a chance to meet

Fernanda, maybe the bond she made with Gemma would never have broken. She would have had the luxury of two mothers."

"I was not a good man, Nonna Maria," Carlo said. "And I don't pretend to be now. I made many mistakes in my life. And I ask for no forgiveness and expect no sympathy. What's left of my life will be spent as you see me. Behind the bars of a prison cell. And that's how it should be."

"Has Assunta been to see you?" Nonna Maria asked.

"She asked the carabinieri captain for permission," Carlo said. "But I prefer she not see me here. I would like her to remember me as she chooses to remember me. Either as her father or as the man who abandoned her mother. She is old enough to make that decision on her own."

"You did more than abandon her mother, Carlo," Nonna Maria said. "You threw her body against a wall in the middle of the night and drove away as if you had tossed away an old jacket."

"And I'll pay for what I did," Carlo said. "In this life and in the next. That moment, that action, will haunt my dreams for the rest of my life."

"And what about Gemma?" Nonna Maria asked.

"She's in her own hell," Carlo said. "If I'd had my way, this whole matter would have had a much different ending. But she was blinded by jealousy, hatred, and revenge. As much against me as against Fernanda."

"Can you blame her for feeling that way?" Nonna Maria asked.

"In some ways, I do," Carlo said. "Yes, I cheated on her for many years with many women. And then I had a child with Fernanda. I am guilty of all that and hide from none of it. But it was her idea to take the baby and raise her as our own. And we had the money to make it happen."

"You wanted and needed that money," Nonna Maria said. "You could have turned your back on it. You could have stood on your own, found steady work, and stayed by Fernanda's side. Instead, you tossed her away twice. Once after she gave birth to your daughter and the second time after Gemma killed her."

"I pray I don't get a judge as harsh as you, Nonna Maria," Carlo said.

"I don't pray," Nonna Maria said. "But if there is truly a God, you will get one twice as harsh."

Nonna Maria turned and began to walk out of the holding area. "I know you are loved by many on this island," Carlo said to her. "But few have seen this side of you. There is a hard heart that beats beneath that widow's black. And you keep it well hidden."

Nonna Maria looked back at Carlo. "To be seen only by my enemies," she said.

57.

NONNA MARIA HAD prepared a feast. Throughout the two floors of her home and the courtyard outside, several large tables were set and covered with white linen cloths, plates, silverware, and wine and water glasses. Platters were brought out by Nonna Maria's designated helpers for the day—her daughters and assorted grandchildren and great-grandchildren. She had worked behind her stove for two full days and had invited thirty of her friends, including Assunta and her daughter.

Pepe the Painter gazed out at all the food, glancing from table to table, drinking from a large glass filled with chilled white wine and sliced peaches. "You have outdone yourself, Nonna Maria," he said. "There is enough food here to cater three weddings."

Nonna Maria glanced out her kitchen window and smiled when she saw Giovanni the taxi driver manning the large grill, cooking what seemed to be an endless supply of lemon chicken. "You might want to relieve Giovanni from the grill," she said to Pepe the Painter. "For every two pieces of chicken he's cooked, he eats one. He needs to save some room for the pasta with sausage and broccoli rabe. It's his favorite."

"And I couldn't help but take in the delightful aroma of my own personal favorite, your famous clam sauce with white wine and hot cherry peppers," Pepe the Painter said.

"Famous only to you, Pepe," Nonna Maria said. "No one else even knows about it."

"My lips are sealed," Pepe the Painter said as he walked off to relieve Giovanni. "At least until the pasta is ready."

Nonna Maria handed a platter of peppers stuffed with breadcrumbs, anchovies, olives, parsley, and capers to her granddaughter Costanza. "Be careful walking with the plate, little one," she said.

"Where does it go?" Costanza asked.

"On the table where Zio Mario is sitting," Nonna Maria said. "They're his favorites."

She pulled three pans out of her oven and rested them on a countertop as Captain Murino stepped into the kitchen. "I came to offer my help," he said. "But I must warn you, I probably won't be of much use. I once worked in a restaurant while a student, part time, as a waiter. I didn't even last through a full shift before the owner asked me to leave."

"How bad a waiter could you have been?"

"I was very nervous, you understand," Captain Murino said. "It was my first job. I managed to spill a plate of zucchini pasta on one table and a platter of chicken with vinegar peppers on another. All in less than two hours."

Nonna Maria reached for a butcher knife and with surgical precision began to slice through the center of one of the pans. "You have to be very careful with this one," she said. "It's three layers, one piled on top of the other."

"I can see the top layer is chicken cutlet," Captain Murino said.

Nonna Maria nodded. "The second layer is eggplant parmigiana and the bottom layer is veal with artichokes. They are meant to be eaten together. That's why how you cut them is as important as how you prepare them."

"Perhaps there is an easier task for me," Captain Murino said.

"There is," Nonna Maria said. "Help my nephew the doctor, downstairs. He's working the ovens, baking the olive bread. Take each loaf out, cut it into thick slices, put them in a basket, and hand the basket to one of the younger children running around. Have them place one basket on each table."

After she had finished cutting through the food in the three pans, Nonna Maria put down the carving knife and stepped out of the kitchen. She wiped her upper lip with a folded handkerchief and looked at the framed photo of her husband, hanging in the middle of the now-crowded dining room. She gave him a warm smile. She remembered how much he loved large gatherings, enjoying the company of friends and family as much as he enjoyed the variety of food.

Il Presidente came up to her, a wooden chair in his right hand. He rested it near a wall. "Sit for a while," he said. "You haven't stopped working for two days. And you haven't eaten anything, just had coffee and wine."

Nonna Maria sat down. "Everything is ready to serve," she said. "I'm letting the pans cool for a bit before we bring them to the table. How did the grilled mussels turn out?"

"They are the best I've ever made," Il Presidente said.

"They should be," Nonna Maria said. "This is the first time you ever made them."

"Sara D'Ambra brought down enough wine to get every guest happily drunk," Il Presidente said. "And Minicucci outdid himself with the desserts he made. The chocolate cream cannoli alone are enough to satisfy a king."

"Il Presidente is more important to me than any king," Nonna Maria said.

"You made these past few days a special time for Assunta," Il Presidente said. "First by giving Fernanda a proper burial, and now by throwing this large party. It won't take away her pain but it will make her put it aside. If only for a little while."

"I did it as much for Fernanda as I did for Assunta," Nonna Maria said. "And as I would for any friend."

58.

THE PARTY WAS winding down and the guests were saying their goodbyes, their hands gripping bags filled with food. Nonna Maria was in the courtyard, sitting at the head of a long table, a chilled glass of white wine in her left hand.

Assunta came up and sat next to her and smiled. "Giovanni gave my daughter a beautiful white kitten," she said. "That was such a wonderful gift. She is beyond happy."

"Giovanni takes in all the stray animals and finds a home for them," Nonna Maria said. "Saint Francis may be the patron saint of animals, but here on Ischia, their patron saint is Giovanni."

"After all that has happened, I began to feel as if I no longer had a family to call my own," Assunta said. "That I was alone. Much as my real mother was left alone and abandoned."

"You have your daughter," Nonna Maria said. "And you still have family. The ones who were here today, young and old, will always be there for you. You are not alone, Assunta. And neither is your daughter. You are with us now. With all of us."

"And with you too, I hope," Assunta said.

Nonna Maria rested her glass on the table and reached for Assunta's hands, grasping them and holding them tight. "For as long as I am alive, I will always be a part of your family," she said. "And I will always be your friend."

59.

THE OLD MAN stood in Nonna Maria's doorway. He had long white scraggly hair and tan skin; a long sliver of a scar ran along the right side of his face. His clothes were shabby. His thin frame wobbled despite the cane in his left hand, and he leaned against the doorframe for support.

Nonna Maria looked up when she saw him but waited for him to speak. She was sitting at her dining room table, a cup of espresso near her left hand, a large pot resting on a thick coaster to her right.

"Are you the one they call Nonna Maria?" he asked, his voice raspy and tinged with pain. "I was told I could find you here."

"You found me," she said.

"I need to talk to you," he said.

"That's always better to do with a cup of espresso," Nonna Maria said. "Come in, sit down and I'll pour you one."

The man took slow steps walking in and eased himself down into the chair across from Nonna Maria. He waited while she poured the coffee. He lifted the cup, holding it with both hands, and took a long gulp. He placed the coffee cup back on the table and smiled. "You make it strong," he said. "Been a while since I've had one that strong and that good."

"It's good for the heart," Nonna Maria said.

"I don't have much time," the man said.

"To do what?" Nonna Maria asked.

"To live," the man said. "Weeks, with luck. Days more likely."

"My nephew is a doctor," Nonna Maria said. "I can send for him."

"I didn't come to the island to see a doctor," the man said. "I came here to see you. To warn you."

"About what?"

"The man who told me about you also told me you are one to be trusted," the man said. "I'll have to take him at his word on that."

"Do you trust this man?" Nonna Maria asked.

"With my life," the man said.

"Then that is all you need," Nonna Maria said. "So, what did you come to warn me about?"

"You have a friend, a good friend, who is in grave danger," the man said. "He has been marked for death. The ones who want him dead haven't made any attempts yet. But they will soon."

"How do you know this?" Nonna Maria asked.

"I was one of the ones asked to kill him," he said. "But I passed for two reasons. One you can see for yourself."

"And the other?" Nonna Maria asked.

"His father saved my life, many years ago," the man said.

"Given that, I didn't think killing his son would be a pleasant way to return the courtesy."

"Why were you given my name?" Nonna Maria asked. "This seems more a matter for the carabinieri."

"That's the last place I would go," the man said. "They would never believe me, first of all. And would probably arrest me as soon as they heard my name."

"So, you are a criminal?" Nonna Maria said.

"I was," the man said. "These days I'm not much of anything. That's why I came to you. I'm leaving your friend's life in your hands. I'm trusting you not to let him down."

"You haven't told me my friend's name," Nonna Maria said.

"Before I do, there's something else I need to tell you," the man said. "By helping him, you will be putting your own life in danger. The people coming after him will not blink at killing an old woman any more than they would swat away a fly."

"At my age, that is not a big worry," Nonna Maria said. She reached for the espresso pot and poured them each a second cup. She raised the cup to her face and looked at the man. "But if I'm to help him, I need to know his name."

"Murino," the man said. "Paolo Murino. The carabinieri captain assigned here. If nothing is done, he will be dead before the week is out."

Nonna Maria rested her cup on the table. She sat back in her chair and stared at the man sitting across from her. She sat quietly for a few moments. "Tell me everything you know about the ones who want him dead," she said.

"You're an old woman," the man said. "And these are hard and brutal men. I hope I was steered to the right person. I hope you are the one who can help your friend."

Nonna Maria leaned forward, resting both arms on the table. "I always help my friends," she said. "Always."

ACKNOWLEDGMENTS

ONCE AGAIN, THIS book would not have been possible were it not for the real Nonna Maria. Writing about the fictional Nonna Maria has once again allowed me to spend many warm hours in her company. I love her more with each passing day.

To my many friends and family on the island of Ischia, a special place I have been fortunate to visit since I was fourteen, I can never thank you enough for your help, friendship, and love. Prime among them is my cousin, the real Paolo Murino. His many emails filled with the history of our family and that of the island itself have been valuable guides in the writing of the first two Nonna Maria novels. *Grazie, cugino.*

To Giovanni, Branka, Antonio, Sara, Angela, Enzo, Salvatore, Pepe, Mario, Gianluigi, Gaspare, Leo, Louisa, and Aldo—thank you for making me a part of your life and sharing your many stories. The wonderful staff of the Grand Excelsior Hotel has become a second family to me and has made their hotel a warm home whenever I visit the island.

To Thomas Augsberger, thank you for embracing Nonna Maria and then bringing her to the attention of the Leone Film Group. And to Raffaella Leone, thank you for loving Nonna Maria as much as I do—her stories could not be in better hands.

To Lou Pitt, for the hard work and the devotion and the love; to Ralph Brescia, for listening and caring; to P. J. Barry, for the friendship; and to Jake Bloom, for all that you mean to me.

I wish to thank the folks who embraced Nonna Maria and passed that love on to friends and neighbors. Among them: Kathleen Neville and the wonderful folks in Wilson, New York—the community library in that beautiful town should be a model for all others; Susan Williamson of Booksy Galore, champion bookseller of Westchester County; Eileen Cosentino and the terrific folks at the Burning Tree Country Club; Ernie Del Negro (and her terrific son, Matthew) of Pound Ridge, New York; Christine Freglette of the BookMark Shoppe in Bay Ridge, Brooklyn, home to the coolest book club in New York City; and Robbie Scott for that wonderful and memorable luncheon in Charleston, South Carolina. Your passion and hard work helped Nonna Maria make a number of new and valued friends.

Adriana Trigiani and Lisa Scottoline, two of our finest and most gifted authors, have always been in my corner, passing the word and willing to help in any way. They have both won my heart. Now they have Nonna Maria's as well.

And a warm thank-you to Jeffery Deaver, Hank Phillippi Ryan, Steve Berry, Camilla Trinchieri, Tess Gerritsen, Robert Crais, and John Clarkson for the many kind words. I will always cherish them.

I am now working on my sixth book with my editor, Anne Speyer, and with each one she continues to amaze with her skill and passion and respect for the story and the characters. She makes our books a pure pleasure to work on, and I can never thank her enough. And a tip of the hat to Jesse Shuman, who is always there ready to do whatever needs to be done to make it easier for all involved.

To my Ballantine/Bantam family—thank you, as always, for giving me a warm home all these years. Kara Welsh and Jennifer Hershey, there is a meal and a cold bottle of wine waiting for you anytime you're in Ischia. And thank you to Gina Centrello, a great publisher and a friend who will always have my heart.

Thanks to Andrea Blatt—a terrific agent and good friend who embraced Nonna Maria from the start. I'm lucky to have you in my corner.

To the gang that gets the word out and works so hard and puts up with my many emails: Allison, Katie, Sarah, Kim, Emma—many thanks from both me and Nonna Maria.

To my friends who are always there to listen and offer a kind word or, even better, a glass of wine: Dr. George Lombardi, Hank Gallo, Peter and Carol Barry, Barry Levinson, Larry Zilavy, Dr. Michael Cantor, Joe Roth, Anthony Cerbone, Guido and Dorothy Bertucci, Leah Rozen, Ida Cerbone, and Joe Lisi—thanks for looking out for me.

As always, a warm embrace to the fabulous Keating family; it would be impossible to find a more loving and caring group. To Mary Ellen Keating, for her love, warm heart, great laugh, and mountain of affection. And for always being there. She's a true treasure and I'm blessed to have her in my life.

To the new addition to the crew: Rocco, an English Bulldog puppy who has quickly won everyone's love and proven to be a great writing partner. He also loves to have me read to him, especially if it's a John Grisham novel. And a shout-out from both of us to Mary Ellen and Rose for taking such good care of him while I was away in Ischia. He loves you both.

And don't worry, Gus, you are still the center of my heart.

To my two grown children, Kate and Nick, both of whom love Ischia as much as I do. Nick has traveled with me there these past few summers and was a great note taker and treated me to many a memorable meal. Kate is a wonderful mom, a terrific wife (made easier by marrying my first-class son-in-law, Clem Wood, who loves her back in equal measure), and a kind and loving woman. They are both so very easy to love, and they make their mom proud each and every day.

To my grandson, Oliver Lorenzo Wood, you never fail to bring a smile to my face and fill me with feelings of joy and love. I love you, Little Man, and always will.

And, finally, this was a time where I was forced to say goodbye to too many friends and loved ones: Vincenzo Cerbone, Sabrina Bertucci, Anna Lo Manto, Max, Sonny Grosso, Mr. G., Rocco, Andy Kay. I love you all and will remember you for as long as I live.

ABOUT THE AUTHOR

LORENZO CARCATERRA is the number one *New York Times* bestselling author of *A Safe Place, Sleepers, Apaches, Gangster, Street Boys, Paradise City, Chasers, Midnight Angels, The Wolf, Tin Badges, Payback, Three Dreamers,* and *Nonna Maria and the Case of the Missing Bride.* He is a former writer/producer for *Law & Order* and has written for *National Geographic Traveler, The New York Times Magazine,* and *People* magazine, among other publications. He lives in New York City with Rocco, his English bulldog, and is at work on his next novel.

lorenzocarcaterra.com

ABOUT THE TYPE

This book was set in Fournier, a typeface named for Pierre-Simon Fournier (1712–68), the youngest son of a French printing family. He started out engraving woodblocks and large capitals, then moved on to fonts of type. In 1736 he began his own foundry and made several important contributions in the field of type design; he is said to have cut 147 alphabets of his own creation. Fournier is probably best remembered as the designer of St. Augustine Ordinaire, a face that served as the model for the Monotype Corporation's Fournier, which was released in 1925.